The Billionaire and I

AN ESCORT AND CEO ROMANCE

THE VENTURE CAPITAL TRILOGY
BOOK ONE

LEIGH JAMES

The Billionaire and I

Book One

The Venture Capital Trilogy

Copyright © 2024 by Leigh James.

Published by Gemini Press.

All Rights Reserved. No part of this book may be reproduced, scanned, or distributed in any printed or electronic form without permission. This is a work of fiction. Names, characters, business, events and incidents are the products of the author's imagination. Any resemblance to actual persons, living or dead, or actual events is purely coincidental.
v.amz.1.10.2023.

This book is for everyone who, like Jenny, hasn't quit on themselves.
You're worthy. You mean something.
Every single one of us matters.
Keep shining your light! ♥
xoxo,
Leigh

Contents

1. Cole — 1
2. Jenny — 5
3. Cole — 8
4. Jenny — 14
5. Cole — 21
6. Jenny — 27
7. Cole — 32
8. Jenny — 39
9. Cole — 50
10. Jenny — 59
11. Jenny — 68
12. Cole — 81
13. Cole — 93
14. Jenny — 102
15. Cole — 111
16. Jenny — 123
17. Cole — 135
18. Jenny — 143
19. Cole — 156
20. Cole — 162
21. Jenny — 171
22. Cole — 177
23. Jenny — 189
24. Cole — 197
25. Jenny — 207
26. Cole — 218
27. Jenny — 228

28. Cole	236
29. Jenny	246
30. Cole	253
31. Jenny	263
32. Cole	275
33. Jenny	287
About the Author	297
Also by Leigh James	299

CHAPTER 1
Cole

"You have to work on their defense." I scowled as the hockey players skated past us, getting beat back to the net once again. The other team scored, and I cursed under my breath.

"They need more training. That guy looks winded." I pointed to our newest wing. "Tell him he's doing sprints, or he's getting cut."

The coach blinked at me. I'd hired him a few months ago to manage my hockey team, the Rhode Island Thunder, right after I'd fired the last coach.

"We just paid top-dollar for that trade. You want me to threaten to cut him?" he asked.

"Yes. Yes, I do. You aren't getting the results I'm looking for." I turned my scowl toward him. "I'm going to be busy for the next week—my best friend's brother's getting married. When I get back, this defense better be crushing it. Otherwise, you can start looking for a new job, too."

His shoulders slumped. He'd probably heard I was a prick to work for—and the rumors were true. "Yes, Mr. Bryson. I won't let you down."

"If you do, it won't be for long." I turned on my heel and almost ran smack-dab into my personal assistant, Shirley. As usual, she was in a rush, and she was also frowning at me.

"Why do I have the feeling I'm about to be chastised?"

Her frown deepened. Shirley was in her early sixties, with blond corkscrew curls, broad shoulders, and athletic legs. She did a lot of running around on my behalf. "You're doing it again."

"Doing what?" But I knew what she was going to say.

"Being a dick." She peered over my shoulder at the coach, who was white as a sheet as he watched the hockey scrimmage. "That's the third coach you've hired in the past year. You need to give him a chance."

"I *need* to win a championship." A defensive tone crept into my words. I tugged at my collar.

"You *need* to let the man do his job. Or at least try to do it," she admonished.

Shirley was the only woman in the world who talked to me like that. She gave it to me straight. That's why

Shirley had been my assistant for over ten years. She was the only employee and the only woman in my life to have lasted that long.

"I'm giving him a chance. And some notes." I shrugged. Sometimes, when I spoke to Shirley, I felt like a petulant teenager talking to my disapproving mom—but I wasn't because my mother was dead. She had been for a long time.

"Fine, fine." Her frown disappeared, replaced by an eager look. "Did you find a date for Todd's wedding yet?"

"No. And I told you—I'm going solo. I'm sure I'll find plenty of new 'friends' at the reception to keep me company." I waggled my eyebrows.

Shirley sighed. She considered it her duty in life to see me married off. "When're you going to meet a nice girl and settle down, huh?"

"Never!" I grinned. "How else am I going to keep you busy?"

"I'm plenty busy!" She followed me through the arena, keeping pace with my long strides. "Plenty busy trying to keep you out of trouble and find you a wife!"

"Who needs a wife when you have a life? That's from *Sex and the City*, by the way." I chuckled.

"I know where it's from!" Shirley sounded exasperated. "And you should not be taking dating advice from an HBO show! Heaven help me."

She was behind me, so I couldn't see her, but I knew Shirley well enough to know she was crossing herself.

"Fair enough." I wasn't taking dating advice from an HBO show, and I wasn't taking dating advice from Shirley, either. I was Cole Bryson, billionaire and ladies' man. I was doing just fine by myself, thank you very much. I was winning the game of life.

What more could a guy want?

CHAPTER 2
Jenny

"You need to get over here, *stat*," Elena growled over the phone. Elena was a madam, and she was also my boss. "I'm packing Dre for an important assignment, and you have to encourage her. You know what she's like."

"She's my best friend, so yeah, I know what she's like," I said. "Stop picking on her!"

My friend Audrey—Dre, for short—had recently gotten fired from AccommoDating, Inc., the escort agency where we both worked. Elena had stopped giving her assignments after she ran out on some client who'd given her the heebie-jeebies. Apparently, Elena was giving Dre another chance.

"The client is James Preston," Elena said. "He's a real-estate mogul and billionaire. Dre *cannot* mess this up for us. This could be a game-changer."

"She's going to do great. Just don't make her nervous!" Audrey was a good girl, which didn't really match up with being an escort. Sometimes, if she got nervous, she did things Elena didn't like. Like pepper-spraying a client because he threatened to lock her up and hate-fuck her. You really shouldn't pepper-spray the Johns. Even the kinky ones. They didn't like it, and an unhappy client could get you fired!

The madam sighed. "Just come to the office, Jenny. You've been getting some calls, anyway. I need you back to work." She hung up before I could protest.

I quickly threw on a dress, brushed my teeth, put on some lip gloss, and fluffed my hair. Then I locked up, which was a production. I lived on the first floor of a shitty building in Roxbury, a tough neighborhood in Boston. Even though it was summer, I closed all the windows and put wooden rods in the sills to prevent break-ins. The rods didn't exactly work, but they were at least something. Then I pulled down the cheap blinds so people couldn't look inside. Even though I couldn't always pay my electric bill, I clicked on the TV so it blared and turned on every light.

If I weren't gone so much, I'd get a dog for protection. Probably a Pitbull or a Rottie, and then maybe a fat, fluffy mutt of a sidekick to be its BFF. But I could barely afford rent, utilities, and my own food, and even though I was usually broke, I still worked all the time. So, I had no business getting a pet.

I grabbed my keys, my mace, and my bag. It wasn't a long walk to AccommoDating's office, which was located in the cheerful, upscale South End of Boston. It didn't take long to leave my crappy apartment behind and find myself in another world. In this world, I was every man's fantasy; I could borrow all the nice clothes I wanted, and I never got eviction notices taped to my door. I could pretend to be somebody else.

I took one last look around my apartment. It wasn't nice, but it was mine. I kept it real clean. The bed was always neatly made, my plants were well-tended, and I vacuumed like three times a day.

It wasn't much, but it was something. *You are taking care of yourself.* I hugged myself for emphasis, which was this weird thing I did when I was alone. *You got this, Jenny. Go help your friend.*

I squared my shoulders, locked up, and headed to work. My friend and my boss needed me, and that made me feel good.

I was something. I was somebody.

No matter what I'd been told all my life.

CHAPTER 3
Cole

I WASN'T HAPPY WHEN MY FATHER CALLED AND asked me to come to his office. Then again, I wasn't ever happy when he contacted me. My workaholic, CEO, multi-billionaire father wasn't exactly the warm-and-fuzzy type.

I eased my Porsche into the parking garage below his building in the Financial District. Dad was seventy-three, but you'd never know it. He had no plans to retire from commercial real estate. He was still at his desk every day, barking orders, making deals, and intermittently watching YouTube videos about how to improve his golf swing.

"Hi Cole." His long-suffering assistant, Kevin, gave me a wry smile. "He's waiting for you."

"Lucky me."

Kevin laughed. "He's on his third cup of coffee, so

watch out." My father's irritability increased with caffeine, but he refused to quit. Typically, by his third cup, he was yelling at the staff to bring him documents he already had and barking about his lunch reservations.

God bless Kevin. I had no idea how he'd survived so many years working for my old man.

I went into the office, which had a commanding view of the city that reached all the way to the Seaport. There were boats in the Boston Harbor, and people were having fun and enjoying the fine summer weather. But here was my father, who had all the money in the world, with shirt sleeves rolled up, a set of architectural plans spread out on the desk in front of him, and a sour look on his face. "Son."

"Dad." I flopped into one of the armchairs facing his desk. "You summoned me? What's up?"

He jabbed a finger at the plans on his desk. "Your guy Ramos is screwing me on this. I can't get the approvals and it's holding me up."

"He's not my guy, and it's not my problem." My father had zero boundaries when it came to business. He was always demanding favors. I was a venture capitalist, so I knew a lot of people. Many of the people I worked with were from a younger generation, one my father wasn't as familiar with.

Dad was always trying to leverage my connections to

his advantage. He wasn't above throwing my name around to try to get permits, special pricing, or other favors, even though I refused to ever use his. There was a reason for that, and it wasn't just that I'd always wanted to make my own way in the world. My dad had a reputation for being a miserable prick—his name might open a few doors, but it closed some, too.

Dad raised his finger and now jabbed it in my direction. "You know Ramos. I want you to call him and tell him to stop blocking me."

"I'm not going to do that. If Ramos hasn't given you the approvals yet, it's probably because the plans don't comply with the newest ordinance."

Dad's face started to get red. *Uh-oh.* "Don't tell *me* about the 'newest ordinance.' You think I don't know the fucking city code? Who do you think you're talking to?"

"I think I'm talking to you, Dad." I sighed. "And I'm not trying to start a fight. I'm just being honest."

"Since when? Since you started your VC company and acted like you built it yourself, instead of admitting that *Daddy* put you through Wharton and gave you every single Goddamned thing you have? Remember that 'Forty Under Forty' article, the one where you said you were self-made? Ha!" He snorted.

"Of course I remember. It's not like you let a month

go by without mentioning it." I'd made the mistake of being quoted for a *Boston Magazine* article. I said that I'd built my company from the ground up, which was true. Of course, I was also the son of a billionaire. I'd been born with every advantage, every connection, and my father never let me forget about it—especially when he wanted something from me. "Apparently, I'm supposed to mention you every time I speak. Sorry I left you and your empire out of one sentence."

"You should be." Dad's face was still red. "I expect you to help me the way that I've always helped you. Call your friend. Tell him to give me the approvals."

In my late thirties, I'd found myself running out of patience. "Or what?" I asked, challenging him.

The finger jabbed toward me again. "Or I'll make your life hell."

"Gee, thanks. Remind me the next time you call not to pick up." I hauled my ass from the chair and headed for the door.

"Just remember who you are and where you came from." His tone had gone from angry to self-assured. My father was a man who always got what he wanted, no matter what the cost. He'd been bully-buying his way through life for as long as I could remember.

"It's not like I can forget," I said as I closed the door behind me.

I wished I could. Man, he was such a dick.

Kevin was nowhere to be found—he was probably hiding from my father. I didn't blame him. I checked my phone on my way out. There was a text from Shirley, who always kept me organized.

> Don't forget you have drinks tonight for Todd Preston—8pm.

Thank God. I would have several drinks and find a gorgeous woman to make me forget about my father and his long list of demands.

Still, I would make the call to Ramos for him. Not because I wanted to please him or because I was afraid of him—I was long past both of those things. I barely felt anything for my father other than the occasional headache. On a deeper level, I understood that he was, at least in part, responsible for my success. I wouldn't be a billionaire without him. I wouldn't have started my VC company from a place of strength. As much of a prick as my father often was, he still opened more doors than he closed for me. I was *just* self-aware enough to realize that.

Also, there was the fact that I was poised to inherit his multi-billion-dollar empire. That had something to do with me answering his calls. I didn't like to think about it, so I chose not to. But in the back of my mind, the Bryson billions were, of course, a consideration. A pile of money that large was the elephant in the room that I would continue to be aware of and also ignore.

I would do him a favor to get him off my back. If he was satisfied, he would leave me alone.

And I couldn't ask for more than that.

CHAPTER 4
Jenny

I HUSTLED INTO ACCOMMODATING. THE OFFICE was bright, cheery, and immaculate, the perfect place to get ready and pretend to be a new person for the next John. Elena kept the place stocked with tons of designer clothes and high-end makeup, all the better for us girls to dress up like every man's fantasy. Hooking was not my dream job, but I did appreciate the fancy dresses and shoes. I cleaned up real nice—so did all the girls.

We AccommoDating escorts were pretty hot, if I did say so myself. And I did!

I burst into the entrance and almost fell over when I saw the guy waiting in the lobby. *Holy shit!* This *had* to be Dre's new assignment, James Preston, aka her Daddy Megabucks Billionaire John. He was freaking gorgeous, tall with thick, brown hair and chiseled features. He wore a custom-tailored suit that looked like it cost as much as a South-End condo.

Looked like Dre was about to hit the jackpot!

I blew past him as he looked up at me, surprised, but I didn't stop. I had to find Audrey. I burst into the office, breathing hard. "Dre. *Dre!*"

"Jenny?" She looked concerned as I collided with her.

"OmiGod, *Dre.* James Preston is out front! And he's frickin' gorgeous! Can I switch with you? Please? You can have Fat Vinnie, and Loopsy, and all my other regulars, but I'm not kidding you, you're gonna die when you see him—"

"Jenny, I'm gonna die if you don't stop talking so fast," she said, laughing. She grabbed my hand and squeezed it. "Okay? You okay?"

I exhaled a shaky breath and nodded. "But I am not kidding you, Dre, you're gonna frickin' *die.* He's that hot. I cross my heart and swear to God. My underwear is soakin' wet just from looking at him!"

Audrey laughed, but she looked slightly mortified. She might be an escort, but she was a good girl at heart. "Okay, Jenny. I get it. He's good-looking!"

I stared at her expectantly. She didn't seem too hyped about the job. "Aren't you excited?" I asked, feeling disappointed. James Preston was the Godfather of Johns—handsome, immaculate, and filthy rich. This was an assignment to *die* for.

"Of course I'm excited," Audrey said quickly. She pulled me in for a quick hug. "I'm just nervous."

"Why?" I blinked at my friend. Dre was gorgeous and smart. She had nice manners and used big words. She was perfect; she had nothing to be nervous about.

"I'm worried about being around his whole family for two weeks, for starters," she said, hitching the collar of her dress. "And going to all those brunches and cocktail hours. Then, a vacation. That's a lot of family time…and I'm pretending to be someone else. Someone normal. Educated."

"Dre, you *are* normal. And smart. You're the smartest girl I know!" I hugged her again. "He's gonna love you. He's gonna love you in that blue dress you got on. You look good, girl. He might even try to *buy* you."

Sometimes, the clients liked a girl so much that they "bought" her. In other words, they paid her enough money that she didn't have to turn tricks anymore. He would then be her exclusive, moving up from her "John" to her "Sugar Daddy." Or her "boyfriend." Or her whatever!

She laughed. "*Buy* me? Like a sweater?"

"Yeah, like his own personal sweater. Don't be silly—

you know what I mean. He might really like you. Enough to not want to just rent you." I slapped her playfully on the ass. "Although he's gonna enjoy renting you!"

Audrey laughed and swatted me away. "I don't think it's going to get that serious. Elena told me he said no sex."

What? I felt stunned, as though she'd slapped me. "Shut the fuck up!" Who hired an escort and then didn't sleep with her?

She shrugged. "It wouldn't be the worst thing," she mumbled.

"Oh, Dre, when you see him? You'll know that would be the absolute worst thing that could happen to you. I'm telling you, he is—"

"Frickin', panty-liquefying hot," she finished my sentence. "Thank you. I'm glad you approve."

Audrey grabbed my hands again. "Listen, I'm not gonna be able to talk to you for the next two weeks. I'm gonna miss you. You have to take care of yourself—don't let Loopsy push you around. I mean it."

I had a bunch of regular clients, one of whom was Loopsy. He wasn't my favorite—he had an unpleasant body odor and sagging balls. Sometimes, when he drank, he got nasty. But he paid, so I never said no to taking a date with him.

There was a knock on the door, and Elena poked her

head in. "Dre, Mr. Preston is ready for you. Jenny, Loopsy's called for you. Twice."

"Tell him I don't want to see him and his nasty, saggy balls." *I'd rather have a billionaire like Dre!*

The madam frowned. "Just kidding, Elena!" I said quickly. It was almost the first of the month, and I had to pay rent. "Tell the squirrelly little bastard I miss him—and his nasty, saggy balls."

I turned to Dre and gave her one last hug. "If Loopsy ends up buying me, and James Preston ends up buying you…I'll be frickin' hurt. I mean it."

Audrey squeezed me back, and I could tell she was getting emotional. "I'm gonna miss you, Jenny…be safe." She sniffled.

"I'm gonna miss you, too…but don't be such a baby," I chided, winking at her. I couldn't have my bestie getting all upset before she met her billionaire. "And if he lets you get in there…suck it hard, girl! Let him know what it feels like to have a *real* woman."

"Okay." She laughed. "I will suck it. Hard."

"That's a relief," said a man's voice from near the door.

Dre and I just looked at each other, eyes wide. Then I whooped with laughter, and we both turned toward the door. There stood James Preston, with his steel-blue eyes, dark hair, and massive shoulders underneath his suit.

Audrey did a double-take, and I knew it right then. She thought he was the most gorgeous man alive!

"Mr. Preston," she said and smiled bravely. "It's a pleasure to meet you."

An awkward silence ensued until Elena bustled in, talking to James and getting Dre's things together. I just stood there, watching, wondering if I was ever going to get a billionaire of my own or if it was just going to be Loopsy and his sad balls for the rest of my life. But I wasn't jealous; I was happy for Audrey. She worked this job to keep her brother in a really nice group home, and she was always helping me and everyone else. No one deserved happiness and a little good luck more than her.

"Bye, Jenny," Audrey called over her shoulder. "I'll see you soon."

"Bye!" I called, clapping my hands together. "Have fun!"

I watched as James Preston led her out the door. Then, I crossed myself and said a quick prayer. *Please let Dre be safe. And please let her live happily ever after,* I added for good measure.

Like I said, Dre deserved it. And no one would be more happy for her than me—even if I did get left behind with old Loopsy.

"Jenny!" Elena hollered. "Please call your client back!"

"Yes, Elena," I muttered. But before I picked up the

phone, I crossed myself again. *Please let there be someone out there for me, someone awesome,* I prayed. *If not today, then someday.*

I didn't know if God was listening, but I figured it couldn't hurt to ask.

CHAPTER 5
Cole

I DROPPED MY CAR WITH THE VALET OUTSIDE THE restaurant where I was meeting James and his family. "Take care of my baby." I handed the valet a hundred and sauntered inside. I scanned the party, which was already in full swing. It was a typical Preston family affair. All the guests were impeccably dressed, rich AF, attractive, and athletic.

That's how billionaires rolled.

I saw James across the room. He was standing with a gorgeous woman, someone I'd never seen before. I hadn't known he was dating anyone. She was beautiful, young, brunette, with big eyes. She stared up at James like he was the only man on earth. Much to my surprise, he seemed to be eating it up. My best friend was never one for romance, not that I'd ever seen. He'd had plenty of women in his life, but he never seemed that taken with them.

This girl seemed to be an exception. He was *beaming* at her.

Intrigued, I crossed the crowded room in two strides, then clapped my buddy on the back. "Well, aren't you two just adorable."

"Ow, Cole," James said, turning and grinning. "You don't have to hit me that hard."

"Yes, I do," I said and pulled him in for a quick hug—a move I reserved for the few people I actually counted on in my life. "It's been too damn long since I've seen you." We'd been best friends for almost twenty years. We'd met at Wharton, where we drank, played pickup basketball, and sometimes fought over women.

I usually won. Scratch that—I *always* won. Not because I was better looking or more charming, although I'd like to believe I was both. I won because I could simply outlast James. He would eventually give up and go home. I never would. I'd fight until my last breath. I loved winning; he loved letting me be an asshole.

"It's not my fault you're so busy with your stupid hockey team," James said. He was, of course, referring to my NHL farm team, the Thunder, and the fact that I'd become obsessed with building my roster. We hadn't seen each other in months.

"It's not a stupid team, and you're right, it's not your

fault we haven't seen each other. Maybe it's hers?" I asked, motioning to the gorgeous woman standing next to him.

I slithered past James to his date. "It's lovely to meet you," I said, taking her hand and beaming down at her—much like James had been doing.

She quickly looked at him as if to ask a question, then smiled back at me tentatively.

"I'm Audrey Reynolds," she said. "It's a pleasure to meet you, too."

"Cole Bryson. And the pleasure's all mine."

"Down boy," James said, inserting himself between us. "Audrey's mine. She's agreed to be my date through these two horrible weeks."

"So she's beautiful *and* brave." I reluctantly dropped her hand.

"Yes. She is." He took another step protectively toward Audrey and wrapped his arm around her as if he was worried I was going to poach his date.

Audrey turned to him and laughed. "I'll give you two a minute to catch up," she said, pulling away and handing him her plate of half-eaten crab cakes.

Oh boy.

I observed them, intrigued, as she kissed James gently on the cheek.

"I'll be right back."

James watched her head down the hallway to the ladies' room, a mesmerized look on his face.

"I thought I'd never see the day," I said. "You're in *love* with that girl."

He quickly recovered, wiping the smitten look from his face and scoffing at me. "You just got here," he said. "Don't start being an asshole already."

"I've never seen you look at a woman like that before," I said. I motioned to the plate he was holding. "And you ate crab. You hate crab. You must be totally in love with her."

"Oh, fuck off, Cole," James said.

He put the plate down on the bar and turned back to me, obviously irritated. "I'm not in love with her," he said, keeping his voice low. "I only ate the crab cake to be polite."

"You're never polite," I said. I grabbed a pint of beer from a passing waiter, even though it was intended for someone else. My best friend was in love—I needed a drink!

James sighed and glared at me. "She's been very good to me," he said.

I drank some beer, waiting for him to say more. When he didn't, I barked, "Out with it. Tell me everything and make it quick. She'll be right back, just like she said."

James glowered, but I knew he'd talk eventually. Like I said, I could outlast him.

"I hired her to be my date," he growled.

Huh? "She's not your girlfriend?" I was so confused.

"No," he said.

I glanced back down the hall, where Audrey had disappeared. "She sure seemed like it."

"I just met her this afternoon. I picked her up from an escort service," James said.

I almost choked on my beer. "Shut the fuck up," I said.

"It's true. I couldn't face my family alone, and I broke up with Logan a while ago."

I shuddered. James's last girlfriend was horrible. "Logan sucked ass."

James rolled his eyes. "You don't have to tell me that. I'm the one who broke up with her."

"So this one's just for sex?" I asked.

"She's not even for sex." James frowned. "I'm not going to fuck her."

I gaped at him. What the hell was he talking about? "She's a fucking escort, bro."

"I know," he said. "But she's just for show. I don't want to get involved with her any more than that."

"You can still fuck her. That's why you're paying her. It's about as clear-cut as it can get," I said.

"It's not clear-cut." He shook his head.

We watched as Audrey emerged from the hallway and smiled at James. It looked like a genuine smile. *Not clear cut, indeed.*

"She's gorgeous," I said. "It's a fucking waste, James."

"I'm making it worth her while," he snapped. "Now, please, finish your beer and come over to see my father with us. I've put it off long enough."

"You're the boss," I said. But I wondered if, for once, my buddy actually knew what he was doing.

An escort. Huh. Life didn't often surprise me, but this was a notable exception.

CHAPTER 6
Jenny

I MADE A DATE WITH LOOPSY AND THEN GOT ready for it at the office. I wore black leather leggings, a black tank top, oversized hoop earrings, and spiked heels. I put on more lip gloss, shook my curls out, and sprayed myself with my favorite coconut body spray. I either looked like an extra from *Grease* or a hooker; I wasn't sure. But I'd worn a similar look for a client the week before and won rave reviews. Conscious of the fact that my rent was due in a few days, I was hoping for a large tip.

Loopsy picked me up from the office. He was in rare form, which wasn't exactly my idea of a good time. He wanted to take me out to a bar and show me off. It was some dive in Southie—Loopsy wasn't exactly cultured—one of the few places left on earth where you could smoke inside and not get in trouble. Which is to say, it was a place for drunks run by drunks.

My father would've loved this place...if he hadn't already drunk himself to death.

Loopsy didn't smoke, thank God, but we still reeked of cigarettes by the time he was ready to leave—which was after nine beers and three shots of whiskey. He was a short, wiry guy, and he could've been anywhere between forty and a hundred years old. It was hard to tell; life hadn't been kind to my client. His face was pitted and wrinkled, just as likely from booze as from age. He worked in construction and had a limp from an old injury. He was in consulting now, or so he said.

But Loopsy said a lot of things. And although he always requested me, a lot of those things turned real nasty on me once he started drinking. And he was always drinking!

Some guys hired hookers for the sex; some hired them because they hated women, and some hired them because they hated themselves. With Loopsy, it was a little bit of everything. I'd come to think of our "dates" as some sort of play he had to act out over and over. It was real sad. Our time together always started out the same: he'd have his arm around me, talking and laughing, telling me grand stories about his past and all the deals he'd supposedly done. He'd tell me I was beautiful and that he was so glad I spent time with him.

Then he would get shitfaced. Sometimes at a bar, sometimes at his condo. But what happened next was always the same. He'd start cursing at me, calling me names. Some pretty bad ones—you had to give it to him, he could get colorful! Sometimes, I didn't even think he was talking to me, like maybe he was thinking of somebody else. Somebody who, in his mind, had done him wrong.

Then there was the sex. Or what was supposed to be the sex. Loopsy demanded it.

"Get on the bed," he snarled. "I want to see that body! I paid for it!" But even with my hot lingerie and banging body, Loopsy couldn't always get it up. Nine beers and three shots of whiskey did that to you! Loopsy's limp dick frustrated him. "This is *your* fault, you whore! How can a decent man get it up for a whore, huh?"

I'd like to say that this sort of client behavior was unusual, but it wasn't. Compared to a lot of the guys, Loopsy wasn't even that bad.

Although maybe that wasn't true. I didn't really know. Because what usually happened after that, I really couldn't tell you. I went dark, as I liked to think of it. It was a trick I'd learned as a little girl. I'd taught Dre the same thing—to think of life like a movie. If it was bad, I pretended I was watching it and that it was happening to someone else. If it got really scary, and it often did, I just closed my eyes. Then I could never remember it—*poof!* It was like it never happened.

Instead, I thought about the dogs I would get, the Pitbull or the Rottie and the fat BFF mutt sidekick. I thought about picket fences, well-tended yards, kids playing on a swing set, sunshine, and lemonade. I thought about how my life could be someday, maybe if I saved enough money and found a way out.

Maybe. Someday.

I never cried. I never fought back. I'd learned a long time ago that it was better if I just went away for a little while.

Sunshine. Lemonade. Dogs wagging their tails.

Hooking sucked, Loopsy sucked, and the movie of my life that I'd been watching since I was little sucked. But I wasn't going to focus on that. Rent was due. One thing I'd sworn to myself was that I'd never be homeless again, and I made more in one hour hooking than I would in an entire shift waiting tables.

I had nowhere to go, no one to run to. So this was it.

This was my life.

For now, Jenny, I reminded myself. *This is just for now.*

Sometimes I wondered how, after all this time, I could still be hopeful. My hope was like a little weed growing in a crack on a dirty sidewalk. Even when I tried to pluck it out, as I often did, it grew back.

So I'd decided that my hope was Meant to Be. And no matter what happened, even with my eyes closed, I knew it was always there. And that was something.

In fact, as it was all I had…it was everything.

CHAPTER 7
Cole

I watched Audrey and James for the rest of the night. They appeared to be a couple that was madly in love. They didn't stray from each other's side, and James had his arm around her waist for the entire party. He even had another bite of *crab cake*. If that wasn't evidence of something, I didn't know what was.

James said he'd hired her, and I believed him. But what I *didn't* believe was that it was strictly business. I'd known him for years, and I'd never seen him look as interested in a woman as Audrey. He said it was for show, but my buddy wasn't that good of an actor.

I might have to force his hand a little—just a tiny nudge.

I waited to make my move. The party started to break

up, and James left to get the car. Audrey was finally alone—and I made a beeline for her, approaching from behind.

She turned and jumped a little. "Oh!"

"I didn't mean to sneak up on you," I lied.

"Hey, Cole." She sounded fake-friendly.

"Hello, Audrey." I gave her a wide smile. I made sure it was on the side of leering. I was being a dick, but it was all for a good cause.

"James is calling for the car," she said, sounding nervous.

"I know." I leaned against the wall next to her, blocking our conversation from the crowd. "He told me about you, you know."

She only hesitated for a nano-second, but I caught it.

Audrey blinked at me. "Really? What did he say?"

"I know why you're here," I said. "I know he hired you. He never could stand to be alone with his family. But he also told me things aren't physical between you two. That's why you should come home with *me* tonight. And I'm not saying this to be an asshole—I'm saying it to help."

Her brow wrinkled. "You're not saying it to be an asshole, Cole? Are you sure?"

"I'm sure." I smiled at her. "It's a *business* proposition. You fill my need, I'll fill yours. You come home with me tonight, and I'll pay you your regular fee. And James will still be paying you. You'll make a tidy profit. It's like a twofer."

I leaned closer, waiting to hear what she said. Audrey looked torn. If she said yes, I could tell James she was just in it for the money. If she said no, my suspicions would be confirmed: she was into him.

"Don't say no to a tidy profit," I urged. "You'll break my venture-capitalist heart."

Audrey looked a little sick. "Did James say this was okay?" She seemed to be holding her breath.

"No," I admitted. "I didn't run it by him yet. But James isn't exactly sentimental."

The door opened beside us, and James headed our way. "It's true, I'm not sentimental," he said.

Uh-oh. He sounded pissed.

He reached us and took Audrey's hand. She stared at their entwined hands for a moment, as if in shock, then up at his face.

He was glaring at me. "That was a dick move," he said. "By the way, I heard almost everything you said."

"It's not like I was trying to hide it," I said quickly.

He turned to Audrey. "Are you okay?"

She nodded, biting her lip.

He turned back to me. "*You* are on my shit list."

Bingo! He likes this girl for real. James practically had smoke pouring out of his ears.

I looked at him and snorted, unfazed. "I'm an entrepreneur—you know that. I see an opportunity, and I move for it, fast."

James smiled at me tightly. "You're my best friend," he said, "which is why I haven't punched you in the face. Yet. But for the record, Audrey is a person, not an opportunity. So please do not approach her with any more business propositions in the future."

I studied his face, my glance trailing down to their interlocked fingers. "Why James, I didn't know you cared."

James scowled. "I care that you find someone else to put your entrepreneurial hands on tonight. Audrey has agreed to be exclusive with me for the next two weeks. Please don't get her into trouble—not with me and not with her employer."

He gave me a pointed look, and I nodded at him.

"Call me tomorrow," James said. "If I answer, it means I'm speaking to you again."

I smiled at both of them, and then I winked at Audrey. "See ya. It's too bad James can't share—I'm much more fun than he is."

James gave me one final disapproving glare, then hustled his not-so-fake date away from me.

"I'm sort of surprised you're calling me, James, after your little hissy fit earlier," I said. I'd moved onto another bar and was currently surrounded by women, none of whom were particularly catching my attention.

"I just dropped Audrey off. She was upset," he said.

"Because I asked her to come home with me, and I offered to pay her? She *is* a hooker, right? Because I really wasn't trying to offend her," I said. This was true, but it wasn't the whole truth. I hadn't been trying to offend Audrey, not especially, but I *had* been trying to offend James.

"I'm not sure why she's upset. Maybe because I told you she was an escort," James mumbled.

"Well, she's right about that," I said. "You probably shouldn't have said anything. She was pretending to be your girlfriend and doing a pretty good job of it. You threw her under the bus with that one."

He sighed. "Thanks a lot."

"So she's gone? Did you fire her? Or did she quit?" I asked.

"Neither," he said.

"So why'd she go home? I thought she was with you for the next two weeks?"

James was quiet for a moment. "I think she just needed to be alone."

"You mean she quit," I insisted.

"Is that what it means?" He sounded confused and, more interestingly, upset.

"Sounds like she quit to me." I let that sink in. "So if you two are done...can I have her number? There's not a lot of action out here tonight."

"No, you cannot have her number," he snarled. "I'll text you her service's number—there's a girl there you might like. Jenny. She's Audrey's friend. Go get an escort of your own."

I chuckled. "I know you like this girl. You can try to hide it, but you suck at it."

"Thanks," he said tersely.

"You might want to call her," I said. "If I want her number, other guys do, too."

"Talk to you later," he said.

"If you're lucky," I said, then hung up.

My phone pinged with texts from James.

> This is AccommoDating's number.

> The girl's name is Jenny.

I grinned and dialed the number. I was always up for an adventure. More than that, I was always game for one-upping James. If my friend could have a hot, no-strings-attached fake girlfriend for the next two weeks? So could I. And mine would be even hotter, with even fewer strings.

Let the games begin!

CHAPTER 8
Jenny

"Jenny, I need you to come in ASAP." Elena cleared her throat. "I have a top assignment for you."

"Please don't say it's Loopsy again. He got so drunk last night that he almost fell down." I *wish* he'd fallen, but I hadn't been that lucky.

"It's not." The madam paused for a beat. "It's one of James Preston's friends. He's a billionaire, too. Apparently, James gave him our number. He asked for you specifically—he wants an escort of his own for the next two weeks. He's willing to pay top-tier. This is your big break, Jenny. This is life-changing money."

"Ho my frickin' God!" I jumped up, rattling the sidewalk table at Dunkin', where I was drinking a coffee. The other customers stared. "My own *billionaire*?"

"Jenny, please keep your voice down. Are you in public?"

"Um, maybe." I hitched up my tube top and ignored the women at the next table, who were gaping at me.

"Just come to the office. I need to get your outfits planned. And we need to talk about etiquette—these are very exclusive parties you'll be attending."

"Yes, Elena." I nodded vigorously, even though she couldn't see me. I had no idea what she meant by "exclusive," but I was going to figure it out and quick.

A billionaire of my own. I could figure out how to walk on my hands and speak French for a billionaire of my own! Well, maybe I could figure out how to walk on my hands. French seemed kind of tough.

"Jenny!" Elena sounded exasperated. "I said, can you come in straight away? Don't even go home. He wants you for an event tonight. We need to get you fitted and packed."

"Yes, ma'am. I'm coming in now." I grabbed my iced coffee and hustled down the street, my boobs jiggling in my tube top, zero fucks to give about all the stares I was getting. *A billionaire all my own. Life-changing money.*

Maybe God really was listening.

If there was one thing I loved about my job, it was the back office. There were racks and racks of designer clothes, shoes, high-end bags, and other accessories. We all picked clothes for our assignments from there. Elena kept everything we needed—whether the John liked his escort to look like a flight attendant, a Playboy bunny, or a dominatrix, we had it all.

Expensive clothes from stores I would never dare to enter in real life lined the racks. I didn't care about labels—high fashion was a luxury I couldn't even afford to think about. But I loved playing dress-up. A fancy outfit and a pair of heels made me feel like a new woman, someone with a closet filled with such things and plenty of places to wear them.

Elena had already started pulling "looks," as she called them. Dress after dress in soft pastel colors with high necklines. I scowled at the gowns. "Elena...*ew*! Who are these looks for? The billionaire's grandmother?"

Elena straightened herself and stared at me. Her hair was spiky with mousse, and her maroon lipstick was applied flawlessly, as usual. She was six feet tall but always wore heels, which made her even more imposing. Elena was attractive but not pretty if that made sense. As for what had gotten her into the escort business in the first place, no one knew.

"First of all, hi Jenny. Second of all, no, these looks are not for Mr. Bryson's grandmother. They're for you."

I pointed at the offensive pastel dresses. "I am not wearing that crap. He wants an escort, not a Sunday school teacher!"

"Jenny..." She put her hand on her hip, gearing up for a fight.

I whipped out my phone. "What's his name?"

"Cole Bryson. What're you doing?"

"Seeing what he likes. Ah, here we go." You had to love the internet. All I did was google "Cole Bryson" and "Boston," and a dozen images popped up. Cole was tall, dark, and exceedingly handsome. Every picture showed the billionaire at events with various beautiful women on his arm.

"Ho my frickin' God, he's *gorgeous*! And he doesn't like librarians. He likes hot chicks!" I shoved the phone at Elena and charged toward the racks.

"Hmm." Elena scrolled through the pictures as I tore through the dresses. "I see what you mean. Isn't that one of the Victoria's Secret models?"

"Probably!" My nerves were flaring. Cole Bryson was *hot*. As in smoking, panty-liquifying hot. As in, touch him, and you burst into flames hot. He was tall and muscular, his big shoulders straining beneath his suit coats, with an actor's chiseled features and a shock of dark hair hanging over his brow.

And he was a billionaire.

Ho my frickin' God, indeed.

I pulled out a black dress with a lower neckline. It was pretty but not perfect. "How much am I getting paid?"

"Same as Audrey. Once he told me that James Preston had referred him, I knew we'd get top dollar." Elena cleared her throat. "If you complete the two-week assignment, your cut is sixty-five thousand dollars."

"What?"

"Sixty-five thousand." Elena sounded dead-serious. "Not including tip."

I clapped a hand over my heart. "Are you fucking with me, Elena?"

"No, Jenny, I am not. And can you please stop using the 'f' word so much? The Prestons are a very proper family—"

"Do you actually mean it?" I burst into tears. "Sixty-five *thousand*?"

"Of course I mean it." Elena clicked over to a side table and grabbed some tissues. "Here, dry your eyes. You don't want to be blotchy for the client."

"I k-know, I j-just can't believe it." I obediently wiped away my tears, careful not to get mascara all over my face. "I never thought I'd earn that much money in my life!"

After paying bills, the most leftover cash I'd ever had in my checking account was two hundred and nineteen dollars. Sixty-five thousand might as well have been ten million—it was an impossible sum of money, something I would never even dare to dream about.

"Well, you're going to make that much now." An emotion that might've been pity passed over the madam's face, but it was gone before I could be sure. "And this is going to be quite the assignment. Over the next week, you'll have drinks and dinners at multiple hotspots in Boston. And then there's the rehearsal dinner and the wedding itself—it's going to be the society event of the year. And *then* the client mentioned that you'll be joining the Prestons on a family-style honeymoon in the Caribbean. But don't say anything to Audrey about that yet, okay? I'm not sure it's public knowledge, and I don't want to start a rumor."

I clapped my hand over my heart again. "Are you freaking kidding me, Elena? I'm going to the *Caribbean*?" I had a passport because the agency required it, but I'd never left the country. I'd only ever dreamed of going to an island. "With, like, white sand beaches? And palm trees? And turquoise water?"

"Yes, Jenny." Elena smiled at me. "There's turquoise water."

"No fucking *way*!" I grabbed the madam's hands and

jumped up and down. "I've never been to the Caribbean! I can't believe it! My very own billionaire and a Caribbean vacation! Holy fucking shit!"

"Jenny." Elena didn't join me in jumping up and down, but she at least held my hands. "The swearing has got to stop, please. For the love of all things holy, no more F-bombs!"

"I'll try, I'll try! I'm just so freaking excited! I can't believe it!" I'd always dreamed about taking a vacation to an island with gorgeous water, sunsets, and tropical drinks. And hopefully iguanas—I'd always wanted to see an iguana!

"Let's get you ready, okay?" Elena asked. "I want Mr. Bryson to be one hundred thousand percent satisfied with our services."

"Oh, he will be." I sniffled but squared my shoulders. "He might've been with a Victoria's Secret model, but he's never been with a woman like *me*. I'm going to make this the best two weeks of his life!" I tossed my curls over my shoulder and started going through the racks again, nervous, excited, and utterly determined.

Cole Bryson was smoking hot, but so was I. I was going to be his absolute dream come true, earning every penny of my fee. My future depended on it.

There was no way I was messing this job up.

WE SPENT the afternoon organizing my looks, which were much sexier than the pale-colored potato sacks Elena had initially picked out. I periodically reminded her that although Audrey needed to be prim and proper for all the events, I was twice removed arm candy. I didn't have to deal with parents and in-laws and all that other crap: I just had to be Cole Bryson's smoke-show of a date.

"Where should I say I met him?" I asked.

"The gym," she suggested. "How about that fancy one over on Franklin Street?"

I had never worked out a day in my life, but I nodded. "Sounds good. One of my clients belongs there—he said it was real expensive." Something like three hundred dollars a month, which was nuts!

"And what should I say I do for work—the usual?" When she sent me out with a high-end client, she usually had me say I worked in Human Resources.

"Cole's family is deep into Boston business, and they own several companies. Let's steer away from anything corporate." Elena looked thoughtful. "I think this time we should say you work with underprivileged kids—just keep it simple."

"I like that. Makes me sound real respectable." I nodded. "Now, is it okay for someone who works with underprivileged kids to pack a thong bikini for a Caribbean vacation? 'Cause I never been to an island before, Elena. And I want my ass to see it. All of it. And I want everyone to see all of my ass!"

Elena sighed. She looked defeated. "Pack it, but maybe save it until dark?" she suggested.

I winked at her. "Dark is for skinny dipping, Elena. Thongs are for tanning your ass." I grabbed several strings masquerading as bikinis and some sexy coverups. If the madam didn't want us wearing this stuff, she shouldn't keep it stocked!

She checked her watch. "We need to get out to the lobby. He'll be here in a minute."

"Hoo, all right." Suddenly nervous again, I fanned myself. "You sure I look okay?" I'd changed into a simple black sundress that showed off my curves, black sandals, and some simple gold jewelry. My hair hung in loose waves over my shoulders, and I wore what Elena referred to as "tasteful" makeup—neutral eyeshadow, mascara, a little blush, and lip gloss.

"Jenny, you're a ten. You couldn't look bad if you tried." She straightened her shoulders. "Please call me if the client isn't appropriate, okay? It's a lot of money, but that doesn't mean he can treat you poorly."

I nodded, but we both knew Cole Bryson could pretty much treat me however he wanted. It's not like there was a union I could complain to, let alone an HR department. But that was okay. I never complained. I never ratted out Loopsy, Fat Vinnie, or any of the other Johns who were less than gentlemanly—which was pretty much all of them.

"I'll be fine. Don't you worry about me. I can handle myself, and I can look out for Audrey, too." There were so many great things about this assignment. Still, I was thrilled I would be reunited with my friend. Audrey seemed like too good of a girl for this business; if I was nearby, I could look out for her.

I followed Elena out to the lobby, my insides still twisting with nerves.

Sixty-five thousand dollars.

A Caribbean vacation.

A billionaire all my own.

The door rang, and Elena buzzed the client in. I held my breath, waiting, as his commanding footsteps echoed down the hall. Then Cole Bryson came into view, all six-foot-whatever of him, in a suit coat that strained against his big shoulders and powerful chest. He was gorgeous, drop-dead gorgeous, with chiseled features, sparkling eyes, and thick, black hair.

He broke out into a smile when he saw us. His teeth were dazzling white, almost too good to be true, just like the rest of him.

"I'm Cole Bryson. You must be Elena." He came forward and shook her hand, then turned to me. "And you must be Jenny."

I stared at him, dumbfounded. A funny feeling passed through me, a shiver, and time seemed to slow down. My tongue felt heavy in my mouth. My head hurt. There was something about this guy... It was this weird, physical feeling, sort of like déjà vu.

I didn't understand it. For a moment, I felt afraid.

Elena glanced at me. When I didn't say anything, she leaned closer. "Jenny...?" She sounded like I was an actor who'd missed their prompt, which was pretty much true.

Sixty-five thousand dollars. A billionaire all my own.
Do not fuck this up, girl!

I came back to earth with a thud.

"Of course I'm Jenny!" I smiled at Cole Bryson and stuck my chest out like my life depended on it, which it basically did. "And ho my frickin' God, we are going to have so much fun!"

CHAPTER 9
Cole

H O MY FRICKIN' GOD, INDEED.

Jenny the escort was, hands down, the prettiest girl I'd ever seen in my life. I'd been with plenty of gorgeous women, but not all beautiful women were *pretty*, not like she was. Jenny's was an accessible beauty, All-American, her friendly, open face impossible to look away from.

Her dirty-blond curls tumbled over her shoulders, her complexion was dewy and fresh, and her full, pouty lips were natural and incredible. Then there was her figure. My escort had perfectly round, bouncy breasts—and I could tell just by looking at them that they were real, perfect just the way nature intended. Her body was toned but also lush. She was just so natural, down to the expression of pure excitement on her face.

She'd only said a few words to me, but I could already tell that I'd never met anyone like Jenny before.

"It's lovely to meet you, Jenny. And I agree, we are going to have a great couple of weeks." I held out my arm for her. "Shall we?"

"Yeah. We shall." She grinned at me and took my arm. I was momentarily engulfed by her scent, something coconut-y mixed with a spiciness that reminded me vaguely of patchouli oil. Whatever it was, it made my mouth water.

Jenny tossed her hair over her shoulder and eyed me as we followed Elena from the lobby. "You smell good," she said.

Her statement, so direct and unrehearsed, caught me off guard. "Why... Thanks. So do you."

She grinned in pleasure. "Thanks. I use a coconut body spray. I think it smells wicked good."

"It does." I grinned back. "It does smell wicked good."

When was the last time a woman had said "wicked good" in my presence? *Prep school? College?* In any event, it was refreshing. Jenny wasn't putting on any airs for me, and I appreciated the hell out of it.

She grinned more, pleased. That's when I started believing that the next two weeks were going to be fun. *Fun.* When was the last time I'd had that? Firing the previous hockey coach was the only thing that came to mind, but that was satisfying, not fun. Not the same thing.

I swiped my Black Amex card at the front desk, not giving the hefty price tag a second thought. I would've paid triple. Jenny was worth every cent; I could already tell.

"Do you like Italian food?" I asked, putting my arm around her.

"Love it," she said immediately.

"Then let's go to the North End for a quick bite. I know just the place." I turned to Elena. "Can you have her things sent over? I'm at Fifty Liberty in the Seaport."

"Absolutely, Mr. Bryson. I hope you enjoy yourself." The madam smiled at me with genuine warmth. I *had* just paid her a large sum of money. "Jenny, I'll check in with you later this week. Let me know if you need anything."

Jenny winked at her. "I think I'm all set, Elena."

She snuggled up happily against me as I led her out. We'd just met, but it was good to have my arm around her, her warm body tucked next to mine. She fit perfectly against my chest. With the sun shining on us and my gorgeous hired date next to me, I felt like a million dollars.

Scratch that. I felt like a *billion* dollars. Which, I'm not going to lie, was a hell of a lot better.

My Porsche was double-parked out front. A disgruntled driver honked as I opened the door for Jenny. He yelled something unintelligible, but I smiled and waved. I climbed behind the wheel, still grinning. "I feel bad for that guy. He's *definitely* not having as good of a day as I am."

"Ha! You're funny, Cole." She ran her hands along the interior of the car. "What is this, the Cayenne Turbo?"

I laughed as I threw the car into drive. "You know your Porsches?"

"I know cars, yeah." She had a mild Boston accent, just another thing I found inexplicably charming. I wanted to ask her what she drove, but I wasn't sure what her situation was. I didn't want to embarrass her.

"What's your favorite kind?" I asked instead.

"Hmm, that's a tough question." She pouted, looking impossibly beautiful as she thought about it. "I guess I don't know the answer. But if I could afford any car to buy today, I'd have to go with a Range Rover. 'Cause that's what all the rich bitches drive."

I laughed. "Is it? Is that what all the rich bitches drive?"

Jenny nodded. "I think so. Every time I see a Range Rover around town, there's a hot, rich woman behind the wheel. I'd like to have a car like that." Her cheeks turned a little pink. "Anyway, how do you like this car? It's fast, right?"

"I love it—and yeah, it's fast. Let me show you." I threw the gear into sports mode and hit the gas. Jenny whooped as I zigzagged between cars, more people honking at us and gesturing angrily.

"I feel sorry for those people!" Jenny laughed. "They're definitely not having as much fun as we are!"

Hanover Street in the North End was packed with tourists. I maneuvered around them and pulled up in front of Alfonso's, the finest Italian restaurant in Boston. Even though it was early afternoon, there was a line; people spilled down the sidewalk, waiting for a table. As soon as I put the car in park, a young man in a white shirt hustled out from the restaurant.

"Hey, Mr. Bryson." He gave us a lopsided smile. "Can I park the car for you? Your usual table is ready."

"Thank you, Luca. That would be great. By the way, this is Jenny. She'll be joining me today."

Luca grinned at Jenny, but good boy that he was, he looked directly into her eyes and not at her rocking body. "It's a pleasure to meet you, Jenny. You will dine with us and love it. Long live Alfonso!"

"Long live Alfonso," I agreed, climbing out and tossing Luca my keys and a hundred-dollar bill. "See you in there, kid."

I put my hand on the small of Jenny's back and steered

her inside. The waiting customers gaped as we strolled past them. There was no valet parking at the restaurant, and the usual wait for a table was over three hours. Or so I'd been told—I never waited. Alfonso's was one of my first investments when I started my VC business. Chef was forever grateful that I gave him his big break.

"Ah, lovely to see you, Mr. Bryson," the raven-haired, sultry hostess said. She wore a form-fitting black jumpsuit that hugged her curves. She eyed Jenny up and down. "And this is...?"

Jenny thrust out her ample chest. "I'm Jenny, Cole's new girlfriend. Nice to see ya. Is our table ready? I'm starved!"

The hostess did a double take, but she quickly recovered and smiled. "We have some great specials today. You'll love it. Right this way." She led us through the restaurant, which was luxurious but simple. The tables were large, reclaimed wood, the walls were exposed brick, and candles flickered throughout the room. Our table was at the end, facing out on the action.

Wisely, the hostess sat us side by side. I immediately put my hand on Jenny's thigh, and she leaned into me. I inhaled her coconut scent again, wondering if it was addictive. It seemed like maybe it was—I couldn't get enough of her.

The hostess asked, "Would you care for some wine?"

"Yes, please. The Barbaresco Gaja should be fine."

She nodded quickly. "Yes, Mr. Bryson."

When she'd left, I pulled Jenny's chair closer so we were touching. "Do you like red wine?"

"I sure do." She surveyed the packed dining room. "This place is popular, huh?"

"That's because it's the best. What would you like to eat? Alfonso does a mean risotto..." Our server brought the wine and our menus. Jenny watched as he poured a sample and handed it to me. "I already know it's great. Go ahead and pour the lady a glass. *Salut*," I said before taking a sip.

Jenny grabbed her glass and raised it to mine. "Cheers." She drank her wine in one sip. "Oooh, that's good!" She happily opened the menu while the smiling server poured her another glass of wine.

"Now, what's this..." Her brow furrowed as she read over the entrees. "What the heck is a *Formaggio e Malazana*?"

"It's mozzarella and eggplant," I answered.

"Ew, they could have just said so." Her brow furrowed deeper. "What about *Polpo Scottato*?"

"It's seared octopus."

"Oh my God!" Jenny practically threw the menu at me. "No wonder they don't say it in English—they're trying to trick you! Whatever happened to spaghetti, huh? I thought this place was Italian!"

"It is." I chuckled. "And there's spaghetti on the menu, right there." I pointed to the *Spaghetti Alfonso*. "Would you like that?"

She wrinkled her nose as she read the description. "What the hell is *micro basil*?"

"It's basil, I think. Just...tiny basil."

"Tiny basil." Jenny blinked at me. "That might be the dumbest thing I ever heard."

"Ha! You're funny, Jenny." I poured us each more wine before the server had a chance to come back. "I haven't known you for long, but I like spending time with you."

She beamed up at me. "I like spending time with you, too. Just don't try to make me eat an octopus, okay? That might just be the end of our friendship."

I KEPT my arm around Jenny the whole time we were at Alfonso's. Our meal was terrific. The wine was flowing; the food was incredible, and most surprisingly, Jenny actually ate. The women I dated—most of whom were models—barely touched their food, opting to save their calories for alcohol. It was refreshing to share a meal with someone who actually *shared* it.

"This micro-basil really kicks ass," Jenny joked as she devoured the last bite of pasta. She dipped the bread—the *pano caldo*—into the infused olive oil *and* slathered butter on it. I watched, impressed, as she polished off the final crumbs and then licked her fingers. Jenny raised her glass. "This was so frickin' good. Long live Alfonso!"

I tapped my glass to hers. "*Salut!* Long live Alfonso!"

The server appeared at our table. "Can I interest you in dessert?"

"Absofuckinglutely," Jenny said. "Do you have anything with micro basil?"

CHAPTER 10
Jenny

WE SHARED SOME *BOMBOLONIS*—GOURMET Italian donut holes—for dessert. They were delish. I never ate anyplace as fancy as Alfonso's before, and I was sure that Cole could tell. But he didn't seem to mind. In fact, he seemed to be genuinely having a good time hanging out with me. The billionaire had his hands on me the whole time, rubbing my back and my thigh, throwing his arm around my shoulder. He was pleasantly possessive, making sure that everyone in the restaurant knew I was his.

I liked that. I wondered what type of women he usually dated, and then I recalled the Victoria's Secret model. She probably knew how to read a menu in Italian.

But she's not here, I reminded myself, *and you are.*

We left the restaurant holding hands, and I couldn't wipe the smile from my face. It was a beautiful, warm, sunny afternoon in Boston, the type of day I dreamed of during our long, crappy winters. Cole was dazzling in the sunlight, impossibly tall and handsome in his expensive suit. It almost hurt to look at him.

That didn't stop me.

We waited on the sidewalk while Luca retrieved the Porsche. Cole wrapped his arms around me, pulling me against his chest. He grinned down at me. "I like you, Jenny. I'm glad you're my date."

I blushed in pleasure and also, in a little bit of...lust? He was so damn handsome. "I like you, too. I'm glad I'm your date." My head was buzzing from the wine and having his hands on me. They roamed lower, skimming my ass, and Cole pulled me in for a kiss.

Woah. I mean, *WOAH.* His lips were firm, his grip on my ass was strong. He darted his tongue into my mouth, and when it connected to mine, electricity zipped straight to my core. Cole deepened the kiss, and I started to feel all charged and squirmy in between my legs.

I pulled back, fanning myself. "Woo! Is it getting hot out here, or what?"

The line of customers waiting to get into Alfonso's watched us with thinly veiled interest.

"Yeah. Ha." Cole took a step back and straightened his jacket. "It's getting hot, all right."

He grinned at me. I grinned at him. But a warning bell

was going off in the back of my head. This was all happening too fast. *You are not faking that smile, Jenny.* True, but so what? I was just having fun with my client. What was wrong with a little fun?

Just then, Luca arrived with the car. Perfect timing! I couldn't be dry-humping my billionaire client on the sidewalk in the North End in broad daylight! I mean, I could, but...

We chatted and laughed as Cole maneuvered the Porsche around the Financial District. He managed to hold my hand as he headed to the Seaport, the neighborhood where he lived. It was a relatively new area in Boston, built out with fancy high-rises and a convention center. The upscale neighborhood was a far cry from my rat-trap apartment in Roxbury. As we pulled down the immaculate streets and the pristine buildings rose up around us, I couldn't have been happier that I'd be staying with Cole for the next two weeks.

"Here we are." He pulled up in front of an enormous building that fronted the Boston Harbor. The fancy sign read,

Fifty Liberty.

I stared up at the skyscraper's edifice, which was all white and sparkling glass. "This looks brand-new."

"That's because it is." Cole grinned. "I was one of the first people to buy here. Come on. You'll love it."

In typical Cole fashion, he parked the car right in front of the building. A moment later, a large young man with a thick neck and massive shoulders hustled outside. "Good afternoon, Mr. Bryson. Can I park this for you?"

"You know you're my favorite, Amari. Of course, I want you to park it." He handed him some cash, then patted him on the shoulder. "By the way, this is Jenny. She'll be staying with me for the next two weeks."

Amari grinned at me. "Nice to see you, Jenny. If you need anything, just let me know."

"Thanks." Everybody we met was so nice. Granted, Cole was a big tipper. But people seemed genuinely happy to see him.

We headed inside the Liberty's lobby, and I sucked in a deep breath. *Holy cow.* Everything was pristine white, with soaring ceilings, a massive fireplace, and immaculate couches dotting the grand space. There were floor-to-ceiling windows facing the harbor. "Wow. This place is gorgeous."

The sun was high in the sky, its golden rays glinting off the dazzling whiteness of the lobby. "It's so luxurious," I said. I felt out of place—sweaty, my hair probably wild from the humidity, and red wine on my breath.

"It's nice, right?" Cole said. "Wait till you see the penthouse."

"The penthouse?" But I shouldn't be surprised. Of course Cole had the penthouse!

"Yep. I can't wait to show you." His eyes glittered as he pulled me close, and I could feel his muscles underneath the dress shirt. I also felt him stirring against me, and a little zip of excitement tickled up my spine. What did my billionaire have going on underneath that suit?

I had a feeling I was about to find out.

He hustled me over to the elevator. When the doors opened, two well-dressed women spilled out, both sinewy, wearing plain but well-cut, expensive-looking clothes and trendy eyeglasses that probably cost more than six months of my rent. I'd noticed a lot of the rich women in Boston wore clothes that were plain and conservative—i.e., boring—but still cost as much as a boat. I didn't understand it, but then again, I wasn't rich AF. So it didn't have to make sense to me!

These women were obviously sisters, with similarly high cheekbones, shoulder-length brown hair, and pinched expressions. Cole tensed and nodded at them. He pulled me close to his side. Amari the valet might be his favorite, but these two were clearly not.

"Ladies, nice to see you," Cole said, sounding insincere. "Jenny, these are my neighbors, the Windsor sisters. Florence and Greta."

"Nice to see you, too," the sisters murmured in unison. One wore navy blue, the other cream. They nodded at Cole, but their icy eyes were on me. Both women inspected me appraisingly, taking stock of my outfit, skin, and hair the way only females did. Good thing the sundress I'd chosen had a price tag of six hundred dollars! But it still wasn't up to snuff, I could tell. The Windsors were not impressed. They were Boston proper and wicked rich—they wielded their huge Gucci totes like weapons, all the better to slay me with.

Did I say everyone I'd met was nice? I lied!

"And you are...? Jenny, did I hear?" the shorter sister, who wore navy, asked. She looked to be in her fifties, with a healthy dose of lip filler and meticulously groomed eyebrows.

She slid her designer glasses down and peered at me. She was probably calculating how much plastic surgery I'd had done (none), where I'd gone to prep school (I hadn't), and how much my trust fund was (nonexistent).

"Yes—I'm Jenny. It's nice to meet you." I stuck out my hand, and she just stared at it like maybe I had the plague and wasn't safe to touch.

Finally, out of forced politeness, she limply shook my

hand. "Jenny, it's a pleasure. I'm Florence. It's always nice to meet one of Cole's friends."

The way she said "friends" made it sound like a dirty word. I might not be wealthy or live in a mega-million condo on the harbor, but I wasn't dumb. The dig was blatant: I was one "friend" of many, and Florence disapproved. Probably not of me, probably not of Cole.

I thrust out my chest and smiled anyway. "Right back atcha."

A faint look of amusement passed over her sister's face. She also eyed me up and down, and in a flash, I saw it: a light dawned in her eyes. She suspected I was an escort. This happened from time to time, and in my experience, it was always the women who guessed the truth.

Cole must bring dates here all the time, and usually, they were semi-famous. But I was just young and super hot, with jiggly boobs and big hair. I'd used the word "atcha"—if that was even a word. So either Cole had picked me up in a bar for an afternoon fling, or he'd gotten me through an agency, and she knew it.

Greta, who was wearing the cream-colored outfit, leaned closer. "Did you two meet recently? I haven't seen you around here before, Jenny."

"We've known each other for a while. Jenny's my girlfriend," Cole said protectively. "She's staying with me for a few weeks. So you'll be seeing a lot more of her."

"Your *girlfriend*?" Greta's eyeballs almost popped out.

"That's right." Cole smiled tightly. "I'm surprised you didn't know since you're so nosy. You two are always keeping such close tabs on me."

Greta straightened her shoulders and sniffed. "I beg your pardon. We are not keeping tabs on you."

"Really?" Cole arched an eyebrow. "How about last week when you called the police because I had a few friends on my roof deck?"

Florence's nostrils flared. "You were having a party and blasting your music at three a.m. on a weeknight. The responsible, hard-working people in this building deserve better than that!"

"First of all, it was Friday night," Cole corrected her. "Second of all, you two are trust-fund babies who've never worked a day in your life. So I'm not sure what you're crying about."

Greta's jaw dropped. "How dare you!"

"You called the cops on me at three a.m. I own the penthouse and the rooftop deck and pay triple the HOA fees that you do. It's my property, and I intend to enjoy it—as I'm legally entitled to. So how dare *you*."

Any icy silence descended on our little group. The sisters looked furious.

Cole's smile became genuine. "Ladies, I understand. You're jealous that I have friends, a hot girlfriend, and also that my apartment cost nine million dollars and yours only cost six. So since you are so decent, and hard-working, and unhappy, I have advice for you: go someplace else."

He swept me past them into the elevator. "See you around, ladies. Or, hopefully, not."

Florence's lips were pinched into a white line of fury. "I cannot believe how rude you are!"

I grinned at them as the door closed shut.

"Right back atcha!" I called.

CHAPTER 11
Jenny

GRETA AND FLORENCE LOOKED OUTRAGED. "We're going to get you thrown out of here, Cole Bryson! If it's the last thing we do—"

Luckily, the elevator doors closed, sparing us from the rest of the Windsor sisters' tirade.

I turned to Cole. "I probably shouldn't have said that."

"Oh no. You definitely should have said that. They deserve it—they're notorious for complaining about everybody in the building."

"What's their problem?" I asked.

"They're rich, bored, and think they're better than everyone else." He shrugged. "They're pissed that I don't invite them to my parties—I have professional athletes over all the time, including Chase Layne, the New England quarterback. The Windsors love him. So they're mad I don't include them in my reindeer games."

"Your reindeer games?" I laughed.

"You know what I mean. They're bitter. So they're always trying to get me, and everybody else in the building who has a life, thrown out." He shrugged again. "They're probably interrogating poor Amari right now, asking questions about you."

"Good thing we didn't tell him the truth—'cause they'd be calling the cops on you again." I fluffed my hair as the elevator silently ascended.

"Those sisters need to get a life." Cole frowned. "They serve on every charitable board in the city, so you'd think they have a decent bone or two in their body. That's not the case."

"People don't show the world their real face," I said. "Look at the internet. You think any of those pictures are real? Nah. It's all fake."

He watched me carefully. "You're not fake."

"Yeah, but I am an escort. So you might want to watch your back with those mean neighbor ladies." I frowned. "If they find out about me, it could be a real problem."

Cole shook his head. "We don't need to worry about the Windsor sisters. They can't find out about you. It's our secret, remember?"

I nodded, then promptly forgot about the mean

sisters, being an escort, how handsome Cole was, and everything else because the doors opened to the penthouse suite, and I was too stunned to think. The sunlight streamed through the floor-to-ceiling windows, glinting off Cole's spectacular home. It looked like a movie set. The floors were rough-hewn wood; the couches were leather; the ceilings were vaulted, and a fire magically roared in the fireplace. Everywhere, framing the pristine space, was the glorious view of the Boston Harbor.

I took in a deep breath as if I could inhale the niceness of the place—as if it could cure me of poverty. The penthouse suite was like magic. It was like *money*. If money had a human form, it would be Cole—tall, dark, and handsome. If money were a home, it would be his penthouse suite. The energy of wealth radiated throughout the space. If my plants moved in here, they would probably grow into a jungle or something.

"Holy *shit*!" I practically shrieked. "Are you kidding me? You *live* here?"

"Holy shit, yes, I do." Cole laughed. "Can I show you around?"

He held out his arm for me, and I took it. "You don't have to ask me twice."

The living room, which I'd been gaping at, was enormous. There were separate seating areas—I counted six couches before finally giving up. Who needed that many sofas? I glanced at Cole, who was explaining that he'd worked with the architect and interior designer to make the space comfortable. "You know," he gestured around the enormous living room, "it just said 'home' to me."

I laughed so hard I snorted. "It'd say 'home' to me, too! I'd move into your freaking pantry!"

Cole started laughing. "I guess I sound like a dick, huh?"

I shrugged. "Not really. It's just crazy—who wouldn't want to live here? It's the most beautiful place I've ever seen!"

"Really?" Cole sounded touched. I heard a note of little boy pride creep into his voice.

"*Really.* Coley, are you kidding? You're on top of the world!" I went and gaped out at the water. There were sailboats on the harbor, and a fishing boat with lobster traps stacked on it chugged by. "I could look at this view all day," I mused.

"It is nice, huh?" He came up and wrapped his arms around me from behind.

I leaned back against him. I could feel an erection stirring, and I was glad. I'd almost forgotten that Cole was a client, not a...friend.

Not a *boy*...friend?

I wasn't sure what I thought he was. Still, the conversation between us was so natural that I'd actually forgotten I was on a job. But I'd do well to remember my place. He wasn't paying me to be his pal; he was paying me to be his escort.

"Do you want to show me the rest of the place?" I asked. I was actually excited to see his bedroom—a first for me. I was genuinely curious to find out what he had going on underneath that suit. That wasn't like me; I'd never admit it to anyone, but I never enjoyed sex with my clients. It was just a transaction for me. The sooner it was over, the better.

Not that my clients had any clue about that. I was a great actress.

But Cole was different. A little thrill, a zip of excitement, sparked through me as he led me back through the suite. I was excited to be with him. I was attracted to him. I couldn't remember the last time I'd felt that way about a regular guy. But I knew I'd never felt that way about a John before.

If I let myself think about that too much, it would raise a red flag. Luckily for me, I wasn't thinking about it too much.

"This is the primary suite." Cole gestured to the most gorgeous bedroom I'd ever seen in my life. The bed was enormous, somehow larger than a king, and everything was white, gray, and cream. It had a very zen, luxurious vibe.

Cole turned to me. "That's my bed."

"I see that."

"I'm excited that you're going to be sleeping here for the next two weeks," he said. "It gets a little lonely with all this space."

I winked at him, then reached out and slowly undid his tie. "I bet you aren't lonely that often, Coley. I bet you do just fine."

A flicker of amusement crossed his face. "True. I'm not exactly suffering."

"Nah, you're not." I slid his tie off real slow. He watched me as if mesmerized, his pupils getting huge. *Yes!* The billionaire wanted me. Electricity crackled between us, but I didn't move. I'd taken his tie off. If Cole Bryson wanted something else, he was going to have to come and get it.

Lucky for me, he didn't make me wait. He secured his hands around my waist and leaned forward. I watched, fascinated, as his gorgeous face closed in toward mine.

"Close your eyes, Jenny."

I did as I was told. A moment later, his lips brushed mine. Electricity jolted through me. Hot chills coursed down my body, and heat pooled in my belly. Cole pressed his lips against mine again, his mouth slightly open. *Fuck.* My insides got all squirmy. His big hands roamed my back. He was taking control, and I loved it. His cock grew thicker, pressing against me. *Wow.* Cole Bryson was a big boy. I wanted to get my hands on him, but I waited, taking my time. Cole was in charge, and I let him dictate what happened next.

He was the client, after all.

I was supposed to give him exactly what he wanted.

I almost slipped into the moment—I almost let go and thoroughly enjoyed myself. *Almost.* But on some level, I was still self-aware, still protecting myself, still in control. I always had to be like that. It was my survival instinct. That's how I'd managed to make it in this job.

Cole deepened our kiss, and his hands roamed lower, cupping my ass. *Yes.* It was getting hot in the bedroom! I almost lost myself in him again. It felt so good. I greedily leaned in for more kisses as he squeezed my ass, pulling me tighter. His bulging erection rubbed against me. The heat built, almost scorching me.

I need him. I have to have him...

Cole's hands continued to roam my back, exploring as his tongue found mine again and again. We rocked against each other.

"Fuck, Jenny," he panted as he pulled back. "You're making me crazy."

In response, I nipped at his lips and rubbed his cock through his pants.

"You're naughty." He laughed, but it was mixed with a moan. "I have to take you. Right now."

I clutched at him, my hands skimming the hard lines of his muscled body. "Then do it."

He grabbed my hips and lowered me onto the bed. Standing above me, he stripped out of his coat and unbuttoned his dress shirt. *Holy shit*, Cole was jacked! His pectoral muscles were smooth and enormous, his vast biceps popped, and his shoulders were broad and muscular. He looked like he could throw me over his shoulder and scale a mountain. I half-hoped he would try.

Who the fuck was this guy? Billionaire Batman?

But I didn't have time to wonder. He stripped out of his pants, and I was face to...well, not face-to-face, but I finally saw his cock. His *huge* cock. It sprang out in my direction, right at me, aiming for its target.

I instinctively spread my legs. I was not saying no to that thing!

Cole pulled the dress over my head, and his jaw dropped when he saw me. Not gonna lie—that made me feel good. Real good. I wore a scrappy black lace La Perla bra and matching thong. I didn't know much about labels, but I knew LP was the best. The guys went bananas over it.

"Jesus, you're perfect." He stared down at me worshipfully.

"Aw, thanks Coley." I grinned at him, basking in the compliment. "You're pretty hot, too."

"Ha. This is going to be fucking awesome."

"So show me," I said, my tone challenging.

Cole dove in, all over me, kissing and nipping and groping. He was as much of an expert as I was. My bra was gone in two seconds flat. He kneaded and kissed my breasts, sucking on my nipples, driving me wild. Yanking my lace thong over to the side, he groaned when he touched me with his fingers. "You're so wet, babe."

I reached down and positioned his throbbing cock against my wet, exposed slit. When I rubbed up against him, both of us cried out.

We were getting into the foreplay pretty quick. I never orgasmed with clients—never—but I could already tell this time was going to be different. Something was building inside me, a fire that threatened to burn out of control. He slid his hard length up and down, his tip grazing my clit. Oh my God...

He did it again, and I cried out, my back arching. *Buckle up!*

Part of me was afraid. Losing control wasn't safe for a girl like me.

"Oh, *fuck* Jenny. You're so wet for me," Cole said, sounding smug. He increased his pace, hips thrusting as he slid his cock back and forth against my slit. I lost myself in the rhythm as he increased the speed, rubbing my swollen clit in time with his furious thrusts. I was overwhelmed by him, by the sensation of him possessing me—but I wanted him inside, deep inside. I wanted him to fill me up and drill into me, come inside me, scream my name.

What the hell, Jenny? asked the voice in my head, but I was too far gone to listen.

"I can't wait." His voice was strangled. "I have to take you now."

He penetrated me slowly and then all at once. My eyes rolled back in my head.

"Fuck!" Cole thrust slowly at first, making sure that he wasn't hurting me, and then started to take me hard. My pussy gripped him, meeting him thrust for thrust, grinding onto the base of his shaft.

Yes.

Fuck yes.

Give it to me.

An energy started buzzing through me, my whole body vibrating. I was going to come, and hard. *WTF?* I reached down and stroked Cole's balls, and he grunted in pleasure. He was lost in the moment, the veins in his muscular body bulging as he pounded into me. The more I stroked him, the harder he thrust.

"Babe, oh *babe*—" He exploded inside me, and the fullness from his orgasm pushed me right over the edge.

"Cole—*Cole*!" I screamed his name as the sensation tore through me, the pleasure eclipsing everything else. The muscles in my sex spasmed, clenching, greedily sucking him dry. I flew higher and higher, leaving everything behind as I became one with my body, one with Cole.

"Yes, *fuck yes*, Jenny." Still thrusting, Cole spent himself into me.

I reached the apex of my orgasm, experiencing a pleasure I'd never felt before. I was so high, so free, given over to the gift of absolute abandon. *Holy fuck.* I didn't even know where I was until I came to, breaking back to the surface, my body still undulating with the aftershocks of intense pleasure.

Cole finally collapsed in a sweaty heap by my side. He opened one eye and looked at me.

I opened one eye and looked at him.

And then we both laughed.

"Well," Cole said, an easy, lazy smile on his face. "That was...something."

"Sure was, Coley. It sure was."

He threw his arm around me, then promptly closed his one eye and started snoring.

I STARED AT COLE, watching him sleep.

I'd been doing that for a long time. Too long.

I was Cole Bryson's escort. He *owned* me; I was his. That in and of itself wasn't a problem, although as I'd lain there, I realized there absofuckinglutely was a problem.

The *problem* was that I'd just had an orgasm. An intense one. With a client. And it had been easy, no manual stimulation required.

That had never happened to me before. Never as in, never *ever*.

And... I'd lost myself for a moment. I couldn't help it—the control I prided myself on had evaporated during our sex. That control, that vestige of clarity, was the secret part of me that no one else knew about. Not my clients, not Elena, not even Audrey.

I never let myself lose control of myself. It was the only thing I had left. My dignity, my pride, my sense of safety—I'd let all of those things go a long time ago. When you grew up the way I did, you learned real quick that survival trumped everything else. And survival meant staying aware. It meant not trusting anyone a hundred percent, not ever, not deep in your heart. It meant always keeping a little bit of distance. It meant staying aware no matter what—even if my eyes were closed and I was pretending what was happening wasn't happening. It meant protecting your heart at all costs.

I'd slipped a little, just a *little*, in Cole Bryson's big, fabulous bed. Maybe it was because of his big, fabulous cock, or the fact that he'd made me laugh, or the way he'd casually thrown his arm around me and made me feel like a billion bucks. Maybe it was all the money I was earning.

Maybe.

Or maybe it was something else.

Either way, I knew that I had to be vigilant. I liked watching Cole as he slept. I liked his big bed and his big cock. I liked *him*.

But that didn't mean I was ever going to let myself slip again.

CHAPTER 12
Cole

Jenny was sleeping when I woke up and staggered into the shower. My limbs were loose, my thoughts lazy and slow.

The escort had literally rocked my world.

And I didn't mean just the sex, although that was certainly part of it. I was extremely attracted to her. Our sex had been explosive, natural, and instinctual. Somehow, Jenny knew just how to touch me.

Maybe that's because she's an escort, dumbass.

Maybe. Probably. And yet, it seemed more like we were actually connecting. Physically *and* on another level. Jenny made me laugh. When we'd gone to Alfonso's, she'd cracked me up with her reaction to the octopus. She was genuine, and it was a breath of fresh air.

Everyone I dated was calculating—making sure they

said the right thing at the right time. But Jenny wasn't like that. She said what she thought, and although I'm sure she probably came from a tough background, she didn't seem ashamed of herself. She wasn't putting on airs or pretending to be someone she wasn't—well, except for the fact that she was pretending to work with underprivileged kids and faking that she was my girlfriend. Still, there was something about her. Something special, a spark that I hadn't encountered before.

Easy, bro, I chided myself. *She's your hired date. You don't have to get sloppy over this girl.*

I wouldn't get too attached to her—I knew better than that. She was Ms. Right for Right Now, and I was thrilled that James had given me her name. These were going to be the best two weeks ever.

My phone pinged while I was in the shower. There were several texts from my father's assistant, Kevin. My old man wasn't great with technology, so he often barked at poor Kevin to do his dirty work, dictating nasty messages at all hours.

> Your Father wanted me to send you these messages. My (standing) apologies. - Kevin

> Why haven't you called Ramos? I'm still waiting on these damn approvals!

> No more excuses. So tired of your BS.

Fuck, I'd forgotten about his demand.

> Tell him I got tied up with something at work. I'll call him this afternoon.

I glared at my phone, wanting to throw it into the toilet, or better yet, out the window and into the harbor below. All my father cared about was business. I didn't even know why anymore—he already had all the money in the world. I wasn't sure why I even bothered thinking about the why; he was a lost cause, bitter and angry ever since my mother died when I was a kid.

Ever since I was little, he'd made it clear that he resented raising me alone. He was angry all the time—angry at life, angry at me, maybe even angry at my mom for daring to get cancer and leave us. Anyone else would've remarried, moved on, and tried to salvage what remained of his life. But my father wasn't anyone else. He channeled his rage into his business, as if throwing more money onto his pile of billions would somehow make everything—or anything—better. He sometimes also channeled his rage at me, the son who failed to mention his father in his *Forty Under Forty* article, along with various other grievances.

I didn't call Ramos. Instead, I wrapped a towel around my waist and headed back to the bedroom. We had to get ready to meet James and Audrey for drinks, but I needed something first.

Something to take my mind off things.

Jenny was awake, curled onto her side, staring out the window at the view. She was so pretty, it almost hurt to look at her. Her dirty blond curls tumbled over the bed. Her face, round, smooth, and open, was relaxed as she watched the harbor. Her lips were full and pillowy, just begging to be kissed. I dropped my towel and climbed into bed next to her, snuggling against her warm skin. She smelled like me and also like her coconut body spray. "I'm very partial to coconuts, you know."

"Yeah?" She laughed and played with my hair, still staring out the window. "That's good, because you know I love my spray."

"What're you looking at, huh? The harbor?"

Jenny nodded. "It's a real pretty view, Cole. Real pretty."

"I know." I contentedly sighed as she played with my hair. It was such a relief to be with someone that I could be myself with. Jenny didn't have any expectations of me. I'd hired her as my date. That made it simple. I could be myself and not worry about anything. Usually, the women I dated all wanted something from me—an engagement ring, a fancy dinner, a connection, being included in some stupid social media post. But Jenny and I were simple. We were a transaction, and that made it easy to navigate. I was good at deals. People—women, in particular—were much more complicated.

But not Jenny. Hanging out with her was relaxing, a far cry from how I usually felt with women after I slept with them. I was always ready to leave—or rather, to kick them out. But I was positively gleeful that Jenny would be in my bed for the next two weeks.

I stretched out, relishing the feel of her bare skin against mine.

She skimmed her hands down my chest, absentmindedly running her fingers over my muscles. The touch of her skin against mine was electric. It started getting hot again. My cock stirred, rising to attention, and I groaned. "You might have to stop touching me. We'll never make it to drinks."

"Aw, Cole," she teased, hands roaming lower, "you worried about time? We can do it quick, real quick. That's why they call it a 'quickie'!"

She laughed, and I rolled on top of her, all thoughts of my father's texts slipping away. Instead, I put my mouth on Jenny's, tasting her delicious tongue, running my hands down her smooth, smooth skin. I inhaled deeply, the heady smell of coconuts engulfing my senses.

We couldn't literally have sex every five minutes for the next two weeks...could we?

Jenny ran her nails down my back to my ass, which she cupped as she positioned me next to her sex. Heat surged through me, making my whole body tingle, embers catching fire. I wanted her. Again. I wanted to make her come. Again. When was the last time I truly gave a fuck about somebody's orgasm other than my own?

Never, said the voice in my head. I ignored it, even though it was right.

I palmed her sex as I readied her for me. She was wet again, so wet. It made my heart swell with pride.

"Right there, baby," she cooed, bucking against my hand. "I like that."

I kept rubbing her clit as I notched myself inside her again. Jenny sighed with either pleasure or happiness, I couldn't tell. I didn't know anything other than the fact that we were together again, in bed, naked, and it was the best thing ever.

So... Could we have sex every five minutes for the next two weeks?

It seemed I was about to find out.

JENNY ASKED me to pick out a dress for the event while she showered. I looked through the clothes she'd packed, but none of them were pretty enough. Some of them were nice, even with designer labels. But none of them were quite right. Jenny deserved the best.

I called Shirley, and God bless her, she picked up on the first ring. "Drop whatever it is you're doing. I have a code-red assignment for you."

"I'm organizing the office for the *Forbes* photo shoot!" Shirley sounded out of breath. "I thought *that* was code red!"

"This is code-red-red." I chuckled. "I need you to go to Saks ASAP. I need a sexy black dress, size six, preferably Givenchy. My date will look good in Givenchy."

"Date? *Date*?"

I couldn't see Shirley, but I pictured her clapping a hand over her heart.

"That's right." I grinned. "Her name's Jenny, and she's *wicked* nice. So get her a great dress, okay? I want her to feel comfortable at this party tonight."

"Yes, Mr. Bryson! Right away!"

I felt like Santa Claus by the time I hung up the phone. I'd made Shirley happy; I was going to make Jenny happy. Then I remembered that I had another call to make, and I started feeling like The Grinch instead.

"Hey, Ramos. It's Cole Bryson."

"I know who it is! You're in my contacts list," Ramos said easily. "What's up?"

"I need a favor."

He sighed. "Is this about your old man? He's been a nightmare. He's trying to buy me off so I'll give him approvals for his project."

"First, he tries to buy you off," I explained, "then he tries to ruin you. So here's what I'm thinking…" We talked for a few minutes about another deal we'd been working on, and I agreed to a few concessions if he would consider taking another look at my father's approvals.

I didn't buy Ramos off, and I didn't do anything shady concerning my business. I negotiated. And he agreed to take another look, with no promises that my father would win the approvals. This wouldn't satisfy my father, but it satisfied me that I'd held up my part of the bargain. The rest was up to him.

Jenny took forever in the shower and then blow-drying her hair. I could hear her singing an old Whitney Houston song. She continued to belt it out as she dried her curls. *Adorable.*

When was the last time I found anyone or anything *adorable*?

Never. I don't think I'd ever used the word.

Like most things of a remotely emotional nature, I decided not to think about it. Instead, I got busy reviewing some work while she dried her hair. I put my feet up, feeling more relaxed than I had in years. I read some proposals, enjoying myself. It was pleasant, sitting in my penthouse, working, while the sound of the blow-dryer blared from the bathroom, almost drowning out Jenny's tone-deaf singing. It was nice to have her here. I chuckled to myself. *Jenny gives good relaxation!* She was worth every penny and more.

I'd almost finished with the proposals when the intercom buzzed. "I have Shirley here," Amari said. "Shall I send her up?"

"Yes, please."

Shirley was red-faced and out of breath by the time she burst through the door.

I rose, setting my work aside. "That was fast."

"I know—you said it was code-red-*red*. So I got here as fast as I could." She triumphantly held up a garment bag. "And I got the most gorgeous dress."

"Cole!" Jenny hollered from the bathroom. "How the heck do I clip this dryer to the thingy on the wall? This is too high-tech for me!"

"Don't worry about it!" I called back.

Shirley's eyes were wide with excitement. "Your date's *here*?"

Shirley was the best, but she was also as nosy as the Windsor sisters. "Yes, but she's busy getting ready. Can I take that?" I motioned for the garment bag.

"I can't figure that dang thing out!" Jenny burst into the room, wearing one of my white T-shirts and nothing else. "Oh, hey! Sorry, I didn't realize Cole had a guest. I'm Jenny." Unabashed, she came over to us and smiled at Shirley.

"I'm Shirley." My assistant grinned from ear to ear. "Mr. Bryson's assistant."

"Ah, so that's how he stays so organized, huh?" Jenny playfully swatted me on the ass, and I felt my cheeks start to burn.

Shirley's smile grew impossibly wider. "I can't take all the credit. Mr. Bryson stays on top of things."

"He sure does!" Jenny joked, then honked with laughter.

I guess I wasn't the only one who felt relaxed.

"It is *so* wonderful to meet you, Jenny. You have no idea." Shirley finally handed me the garment bag. "I'm so happy that Mr. Bryson has a nice date to bring to the event tonight."

"Aw, thanks, Shirley." Jenny smiled, pleased, then looked questionably at the bag when I handed it to her. "What's this?"

"It's a dress for tonight," I explained. "I had Shirley pick it out."

"You got me a dress?" Jenny's eyes got big in her face. "Thank you, Coley. And thank you, Shirley!"

"You should go see if it fits." I was ready to get Jenny

and Shirley away from each other before there were more ass-slapping, "Coleys," or questions.

"I'll do it right now. Shirley, wanna help me? I suck at zippers."

"Oh, I'd love to!" Shirley was practically trembling with excitement as she followed Jenny into my bedroom.

The fuck?

They disappeared together, and I heard the two of them talking and laughing. There was a lot of "Oh my Gods" and "That body!" Shirley was obviously taken with Jenny. I couldn't believe my assistant was in my *bedroom* with my *escort*. FFS, I hadn't planned on this.

"Ta-da!" Shirley burst out of the room, and Jenny shyly walked out behind her. She was stunning in the simple black dress with a plunging neckline that showed off her incredible curves. Although the dress was unembellished and black, it was couture. Jenny looked like a million bucks in it.

Scratch that—a billion.

"You look lovely," I said. For some reason, my heart hurt a little.

"Doesn't she?" Shirley clapped her hands together. "She's the prettiest girl in the whole world!"

Jenny nudged her. "Don't be silly."

"Oh honey, I mean it." Shirley smiled at her, then

turned to me. "I should probably get going. That *Forbes* shoot is first thing in the morning!"

"Thank you, Shirley." I was relieved she was leaving, but I was grateful to her.

"Yeah, thanks, Shirley. I really love this dress—it's the nicest thing I've ever worn." Jenny's voice was tinged with emotion.

Shirley smiled at her again. "It looks great on you, hon. Have fun, you two."

Shirley let herself out. Before I even heard the elevator, my phone pinged with a text from her.

It was a row of thumbs-up emojis.

I just shook my head, then laughed.

CHAPTER 13
Cole

Jenny looked like a sexy princess; I puffed up with pride as we took the elevator to the lobby. "You really look incredible in that dress," I told her.

"Aw, thanks." She blushed in pleasure. "I meant what I said: it's the nicest thing I've ever worn. I saw the price tag—holy cow, Cole. I promise I'll take good care of it so you can return it after tonight."

"What?" I scoffed. "We are not returning that dress. It was made for you. It's a gift."

"Wow." Jenny gently stroked the luxurious material. "That's... That's real nice of you, Coley."

"It's my pleasure." I meant it.

The elevator doors opened, and I swept Jenny out into the lobby where, lo and behold, the Windsor sisters were sitting and having a glass of wine, watching the sunset.

Their eyeballs almost popped out when they saw her in the dress.

"Ladies," I said.

"Hey, Florence. What's up, Greta," Jenny said, grinning at them as we passed.

Amari did a double take when he saw how gorgeous Jenny looked, but true professional that he was, he recovered quickly. "Mr. Bryson. Ms. Jenny. You two are looking your best. The car is waiting out front."

"Thanks, Amari." I nodded.

"Yeah, thank you." Jenny grinned at him.

"I think everyone's as impressed as I am with you in that dress," I said as I opened her car door for her. Even Greta and Florence were speechless."

"Ha, I don't know." She shrugged. "At least I looked fancy when I saw your nosy-neighbor ladies."

"Yes, I enjoyed that, too." I smiled as I pulled out onto the road, setting the Porsche's navigation to the party. The Prestons were hosting it at a fancy Back Bay restaurant.

"Shirley seems real nice," Jenny said. "I've never had a personal shopper before."

"Shirley's the best," I agreed. "She's been with me forever. I don't know what I'd do without her."

"You should buy her a present." Jenny nodded. "Like a tropical vacation or something. Or a four-thousand-dollar dress."

"That's a good idea. I usually give her chocolates at Christmas, but I could get her something for her birthday. She always remembers mine."

Jenny scowled at me. "You get her chocolates for Christmas? I met Shirley for ten minutes, and I could already tell that she would do anything for you. She's going back to organize your office, and it's seven o'clock at night! Screw the chocolate. Get her a Porsche."

I laughed. "You're good at spending my money, Jenny! Lots of creative ideas. I like it."

She laughed, too. "Sorry about that. I just think you should reward good people, ya know? Good people are hard to find."

"True, very true." I reached over and grabbed her hand, then held it for the rest of the ride.

The cocktail hour was in full swing when we got there, with the typical well-dressed Preston crowd. Jenny hitched up her dress, then fluffed her hair. "This is a fancy party, huh?"

"Fairly fancy," I agreed. "The Prestons are an old-money family. You'll probably see a lot of Chanel suits and pearls tonight."

She looked confused. "On the men?"

I laughed. "No, the women—Chanel suits are classic Boston rich-white-women wear. I'll show you."

She hesitated before we walked in.

"You have nothing to worry about," I assured her. "You look gorgeous, Jenny. You're the prettiest girl in the world."

"Cole, *stop*. You're so silly."

"I mean it." I grabbed her hand again. "Shirley was right."

We headed for the bar, and I did not imagine it—every single dude in the restaurant checked out Jenny from head to toe. She was the prettiest girl in the world, and I was so lucky she was my date. "What do you want to drink?" I asked.

"Something fruity. With a straw, so I don't mess up my lip gloss." She motioned to her face.

"I'm on it." I turned to the bartender and ordered a bourbon for myself and a rum punch with a straw for Jenny. She slurped her drink down fast, and I followed suit. I wasn't going to let her outdrink me.

I pulled her onto my lap. "We should go to a Thunder game sometime," I said.

"You mean the hockey team?" Jenny asked.

"Yeah—I own them."

She almost spit out her drink. "What? You own a hockey team?"

"Yep. You know what that means, right?"

"That you're rich as fuck?"

I almost spit out my drink. "Yes, but that's not what I

was going to say. What I was going to say was that it means we can have box seats, baby. Would you be my date to a game? There's actually one tonight—if we leave here in time, we can make the third period."

"Coley, I'd be honored," she cooed. "Box seats all the way!"

Picturing us at the game made me smile. I could see Jenny in a Thunder hoodie, drinking beer from a plastic cup, hooting and hollering at the team. I squeezed her against me, vowing to buy her both a hoodie and a beer later. "It's a date."

We largely ignored everyone else at the party. Instead, Jenny sat on my lap while we drank. It was awesome. When she excused herself to go to the ladies' room, I ordered more cocktails. I felt like the cat that had swallowed the canary as I sat at the bar, waiting for her to return and also for James to show up. I hadn't talked to him since he'd given me AccommoDating's phone number. He didn't know I was bringing Jenny tonight. I could hardly wait to see my friend's face!

James and Audrey came in a few minutes later. It didn't escape my notice that they held hands, and that their complexions looked bright. Orgasms were good for your skin. I knew all about that. My complexion looked like I'd had the three-hundred-dollar facial at Balans on Newbury Street.

"I didn't invite you here," James said, clapping me on the back. "But it's nice to see you anyway." He kept Audrey close to his side, probably worried that I would try to steal her again.

Little did he know. I had an escort all my own.

"Todd texted me," I said. "He wants me to come to everything I can. He said he wants to make you happy."

"Aw, that's sweet," James said. He inspected me, eyes narrowing as he looked me up and down. "You're looking smugger than usual. Why's that?"

I beamed at him. "That's why." I pointed to Jenny as she hustled back into the room. She was walking fast and applying lip gloss, her curls bouncing and her voluptuous chest jiggling in the gorgeous Givenchy dress.

"Ho my frickin' God!" Jenny shouted when she saw Audrey. She practically shoved James out of the way to get to her.

"Yay!" she yelled, grabbing Audrey into a hug and jumping up and down. "You got me my own billionaire! I'm so freaking excited!"

"Oh, Jesus," James said. "You didn't."

"Yes, I did. Ho my frickin' God, I did," I said, chuckling. "I'm gonna marry this girl. She's got a mouth like a—"

"Cole," James said, cutting me off. "My mother is ten feet away from us. *Please.*"

"I don't have to finish the sentence, anyway," I said. I watched Jenny hug Audrey again, the two of them talking a mile a minute. "You know what I mean."

He sighed. "I can guess." We stood and watched the girls talking excitedly to each other.

"You're the one who told me to call her," I reminded him.

"I didn't mean for you to bring an escort to my brother's wedding functions," James said.

For the second time that evening, I almost spit out my drink. "You should talk, bro."

James glared at me, but I could tell he wasn't mad. "Buy me a free drink. I need one."

I motioned for the bartender and ordered James a martini.

James leaned closer and lowered his voice. "I'm happy you're here and that Jenny's working out for you. But I need to protect Audrey. No one but you knows the truth. It has to stay that way."

I nodded and slid his martini over. We were in the Preston Viper pit, and James *did* need a drink. His family would freak out if they had any idea about Audrey's real identity.

"Of course. I promise I won't say anything about either of them," I said. "I wouldn't do that to you—you know that. But I have to say, for the hired help, you're being very protective of her."

"She needs my protection," James said immediately. "She's a sweet girl. I know that sounds ridiculous, but it's true."

"It doesn't sound ridiculous. But what are you going to do after this is all over?" He might not admit it, but it was clear James was into this girl.

He shrugged. "Probably nothing."

"That sounds ridiculous," I said. "And I'm only saying that because you're my best friend."

"Sometimes I think I need to protect her from myself," James said.

I was about to tell him he sounded doubly ridiculous, but Jenny and Audrey came to the bar then, still happily chatting. James put his arm around Audrey and kissed the top of her head. I watched him, gobsmacked. I'd never seen him like this with a woman before.

"I didn't know you owned part of the Rhode Island Thunder, Cole. Jenny just told me. That's so cool," Audrey said.

"We have box seats tonight," Jenny squealed. I put my arm around her and squeezed her against me.

"We can have box seats whenever you want, princess," I said, then kissed her on the nose. Jenny smiled at me happily, and my heart swelled again. We stayed like that, arms wrapped around each other as we chatted with James and Audrey.

Several times, I caught Audrey observing her friend. "Jenny, come to the bathroom with me," she said after a while, grabbing her by the hand. She flashed a dimpled smile at us. "We'll be back in a few, guys."

"What's that all about?" I asked, watching Audrey drag Jenny away.

"I think Jenny's going to get a talking to," James said.

I scratched the back of my neck. "About what?"

"Not getting her hopes up about the billionaire with the box seats," James said.

"Huh," I said as I watched them retreat.

Was Jenny getting her hopes up?

And if she was...was that really the worst thing?

CHAPTER 14
Jenny

"I just went pee," I complained to Audrey. "I don't really need to go again."

"Fine. I just want to talk to you for a minute." Audrey steered me past the ladies' room down the hall to the empty coat check.

She looked around carefully, making sure that no one was nearby or could see us. "Jenny," she said gently. "Cole hired you through AccommoDating, right?"

"Of course," I said.

"He seems like a nice guy."

"He's awesome, Dre! We've been having so much fun." I grinned and grabbed her hands. "Thank you for doing this for me. Elena's so happy that James sent her a referral. I told her I was going to rock Cole's world and make him a regular."

"Okay," she said. "I just want to make sure, though..." Audrey bit her lip.

"What?"

"That you don't think he's gonna buy you, or anything," she said miserably. "The way you were looking at him out there—"

"Aw, Dre, c'mon," I said, laughing. "This isn't my first date. You don't think I have an actual crush on Cole Bryson, do you?"

Audrey looked confused. "Don't you?" she asked.

I shrugged. "I like his wallet. I like his thick cock. I like his box seats. I like batting him around like a cat toy."

"You don't like *him*?"

"Oh yeah—I like him, all right. Who the fuck wouldn't? He's wicked hot, and he's a billionaire! But he's a John, Dre. He's paying for me to do whatever he wants. And he wants to do lots of things, let me tell you. He's nasty, and I like it.

"But just because I'm enjoying myself doesn't make it any less of a job," I said. "Or any more than a job. I mean—oh, you know what I mean." Talking to Audrey made it crystal clear: Cole Bryson was a job—one that I enjoyed—but nothing more.

Audrey nodded at me. "I know exactly what you mean."

"Enough about me. I can take care of myself." I looked at Audrey. "How's it going with Mr. Sex in a Suit?"

"Great," she said, but it sounded like a lie.

"He *did* fuck you, right? I saw you two out there."

"He fucked me," she said, sounding miserable. "We fucked."

"Was it that bad?" She looked so upset I squeezed her hand. "Dre, are you going to cry or something?"

"No," she said, but her eyes were totally filling with tears. She blotted them carefully. "Jenny, I can't cry. His whole family is out there. And they can't know how we know each other, either."

"Okay," I said, my professional training kicking in. "We can handle that. I've had to lie to so many wives and girlfriends that the lies just spring out, Dre. And they're usually pretty good. Don't worry about that part. But we do need to worry about those tears. Tell me what's going on."

Audrey shook her head. "I can't. I can't talk about it."

"He hit you or something?" I cracked my knuckles, preparing to go and fight James Preston. "Is he some kind of freak?"

"Nope," she said.

I immediately believed her. But there was still some problem... If James wasn't abusing her, and they'd been having great sex, the issue was that she probably liked him.

Elena warned us all the time that getting emotionally involved with your client was dangerous. It could only lead to heartbreak.

"You cross some kind of line with yourself?" I asked.

Audrey sniffled. "Something like that."

"S'okay, Dre. That happens to everybody." I hugged her. "The thing is, nobody knows what those lines are but you. That's why it's awesome that feelings and thoughts are *invisible*. They're like magic. Nobody knows the truth but you, okay? You're safe."

"Okay." But she sniffled some more.

"So you do what you think is right," I told her. "And remember, if it gets too bad, just close your eyes."

"'Cause then it's like it never happened." Audrey nodded. "Jenny, I probably haven't told you this lately, but you're smart."

"I know," I said. "It's my secret weapon." I gave my friend a long look. "And Dre—just because it's not gonna happen for me, doesn't mean it's not gonna happen for you."

"What?" she asked.

"You know." Audrey should be the exception to the "no emotional attachment" rule. She was a good girl, and she was good enough for anybody—including a proper billionaire like James Preston.

She shrugged. "Jenny, it's not gonna happen for me."

I shook my head and pointed at myself. "No billionaire's gonna buy me. 'Cause I'm a whore, Dre, and I don't even feel bad about it. But you're different. You're doing this to take care of your brother. You're actually a good girl. Mr. Suit knows that. I can tell."

"He's not going to buy me," she said.

"He might." I grinned at her. "Crazier shit's happened, that's for sure."

"What about you and Cole?"

I laughed. "I am going to suck him as dry as I can—him and his wallet!"

Audrey finished drying her eyes, and I linked my arm through hers. "You ready?" I asked.

She nodded.

"Then let's go bat some billionaires around like cat toys," I said, giving my friend a wicked grin.

OUR LITTLE GROUP was quite popular that evening. Everyone wanted to have a drink with the two gorgeous billionaires and their super-hot, mysterious dates. Even Evie—the skinny, bitchy, bride-to-be—seemed impressed.

She and Todd, James's brother, were talking to us. Upon closer inspection, Evie was pretty in a snotty, tailored, Boston-proper sort of way. She was wasted, teetering in her fancy shoes as she eyed first James, then Cole up and down.

"You own part of the Thunder?" Evie asked, her flat chest pressed out toward Cole. She looked at him as if he was some sort of rock-star, farm-team-owning Greek God. And she was totally ignoring the fact that he had his arm around me, his date! Not to mention her fiancé standing next to her.

Not on my watch, bitch.

I stepped in front of Cole. "Yeah, he does," I said. I thrust out my much more formidable chest, daring Evie to come closer.

She was about to say something back when Todd interrupted. "Are you flirting with the best man's best friend?" he asked his fiancée. They were both slurring their words a little; the cocktail "hour" had been going for three hours straight.

Evie tossed her hair and narrowed her eyes at him. "Sorry, baby," she said in what sounded like her version of a sexy voice. "Old habits die hard."

"You mean once a slutty sorority girl, always a slutty sorority girl?" Todd asked, grinning at her.

"That's exactly what I mean." She grabbed his tie and pulled him in for a quick, hot kiss. Todd lifted her up, and she wrapped her legs around him. They headed to a dark corner for some serious making out and grinding.

"They're drunk," Cole said. He turned to me, eyes ablaze. "But enough about them—you are so hot when you fight for me, babe."

"That wasn't even a fight," I said, tossing my hair. "If you want to see me throw down, just bring that bitch back here."

Cole looked impressed. "That's so hot—that's the bride, Jenny. You gonna fight the bride for me?"

"I would, baby," I cooed, pressing myself against him. We started seriously making out then, with Cole's hands all over my ass. Almost getting into a fight with Evie had gotten me all hot and bothered. How dare she try and flirt with my man! Hot pride bloomed in my chest as his hands roamed over me. He deepened our kiss. I forgot all about James and Audrey, all about Evie, and all about batting billionaires around like cat toys.

I was being batted around, and I liked it.

As the night wore on, the party got increasingly louder. It seemed as though everybody was drinking a lot and having a good time. Todd and Evie were still dry-humping in their corner—I was pretty sure the uptight Preston family didn't love *that*!

James and Audrey snuck out a little before midnight. Audrey winked at me, and I gave her a thumbs-up. Cole still had his hands on my ass, just where I liked them.

"Do you want to get out of here, too?" Cole whispered.

"You don't have to ask me twice."

COLE WAS TOO drunk to drive. He called for a private car. Five minutes later, a black Escalade pulled in front of the restaurant. The driver hopped out, opened the door for us, and then whisked us off into the night.

Being a billionaire didn't suck.

In the back of the Escalade, Cole threw his arm around me. I snuggled against him. He kissed the top of my head, then yawned. "It's pretty late to head to the game. Some other ones are coming up, babe. Want to go to one of them instead?"

I'd forgotten all about the Thunder and our box seats. The nine rum punches must've clouded my thoughts. I yawned, too. "Absofuckinglutely. It's been a long day. A long one, but a good one."

"I agree." He kissed the top of my head again. "I agree."

We stumbled into the Liberty, and I was relieved that the bitchy Windsor sisters were long gone. Up in the penthouse suite, I carefully stripped out of my dress, hung it up, washed off my makeup, and brushed my teeth. Then I climbed into bed next to Cole and sighed when I rested my head on his insanely soft pillows.

"This is nice, Coley. Real nice."

He pulled me against his chest and kissed my forehead. "It's the nicest, Jenny. Especially with you here."

Cole promptly started snoring.

Sleep eluded me for a few minutes, and I wasn't sure why. That is until I realized that I was listening to the beating of Cole's heart and wondering if, just if, he meant what he'd said. *It's the nicest...especially with you here.*

Forget about it, Jenny, I thought. *He's just a John.*

As Audrey said earlier, I was smart. It was my secret weapon, and I was not above using it on myself.

CHAPTER 15
Cole

Sleeping with Jenny was lovely, and I didn't mean sleeping with her sleeping with her. I meant sleeping *next* to her.

I never let the women I dated sleep over. As in, never *ever*. As soon as we finished having sex, I was out the door. If it were the unfortunate circumstance that we'd ended up at my place, I'd make some excuse about having to take meetings with my global business partners in the middle of the night. Then I'd call for a car and send the woman on her way.

I never called and asked for a second date. I never texted. I was, as Shirley had once said, about as emotionally unavailable as you could get. But this thing with Jenny was different. She was my paid roommate, so that made her presence "safe." Having her in my bed was expected. It was part of the deal.

I was surprised, however, by just how much I enjoyed it.

The thing was, she snored. She splayed her legs out and took over more than her fair share of the bed. I usually couldn't stand anyone touching me while I slept, but when she pressed up against me, I felt comfortable. Despite drinking way too much at the party, I'd slept great.

I was a chronically early riser. So when I woke up, Jenny was still asleep. Sunlight streamed through the windows and framed her pretty face. She looked so innocent, so vulnerable. Something unfurled inside my chest; some sort of grip loosened its hold. I didn't know what that meant. But I did know that as I watched Jenny, I had this overwhelming urge to protect her. How was someone so sweet stuck working as an escort? How did that happen? I had no idea what her life was like. I just knew that she was funny and beautiful and that she stood up for herself.

She probably has to stand up for herself a lot. It was an unpleasant thought. I didn't want to picture the dark side of what Jenny had to endure as part of her job.

Sighing, I climbed from the bed. I had a private chef who left meals prepared for me; I'd asked him to make double portions while Jenny was staying with me. I padded out to the kitchen, made myself a coffee, and pulled out breakfast from my enormous refrigerator. It was homemade waffles with berries, and it looked delicious. *Yum.* I plated everything, then went and watched the sun rise higher in the sky.

My phone pinged with a text from James.

> Hope you got home okay last night.

> You were pretty wasted.

> YOU were pretty wasted.

> How's your date?

He didn't text back for a minute. Then:

> Good. Stop bugging me.

> BTW, Todd and Evie want you at the Rehearsal Dinner tonight. Il Pastorne, your neck of the woods.

> You stop bugging ME. See you tonight.

> If you're lucky

In typical James style, he didn't respond. I thought about my friend, remembering the way he'd held on to Audrey at the bar last night. He'd watched her every move.

The look on his face told me everything I needed to know he was smitten with her. Big time. The fact that he'd been holding her hand and making out with her in front of his whole family was a big deal. He'd never been affectionate with anyone in public before. Audrey might not know that, but I did.

I wondered if James himself was aware of his feelings. And then I wondered what exactly he was going to do with that escort of his.

"Good morning." Jenny came into the kitchen wearing my T-shirt again. She looked impossibly beautiful with no makeup on, the morning sunlight glinting off her creamy skin and the gold flecks in her hair.

"Good morning, Jenny. Coffee?"

"Yeah, definitely." She rubbed her temples. "My head hurts. I drank too much last night."

"Me too." I got up, made her a coffee, and slid it across the island. She grabbed it gratefully and smiled at me.

I smiled at her. And then I just…stood there. I didn't know what to do. I was suddenly feeling… What the hell was I feeling? *Shy?*

"Would you like some cream?" I sounded like a server waiting on their first-ever table, petrified and wooden. I'd never actually had a woman in my penthouse for breakfast. *Shit!* I didn't know what to do!

"Yeah, sure. Hey, are those waffles?" Jenny perked up at the sight of food. "Those look awesome!"

She maneuvered around me, grabbing the plates and popping them in the microwave. Then she rummaged around in my refrigerator for syrup. "This is the biggest frickin' fridge I've ever seen. You could get lost in here!" She finally pulled out the syrup, triumphant. "Aha!"

Jenny grabbed the plates, clanged through some drawers until she found napkins and silverware, and then set everything on the island. "You want some orange juice?"

"Sure. I'd love some." I watched, fascinated, as she bustled around the kitchen some more. She added cream to her coffee. She poured us each a glass of orange juice. She even found some powdered sugar and set it next to the maple syrup. What was I worried about? Jenny made everything easy.

But maybe that, in and of itself, was something to worry about. I decided not to think about it. Instead, I sat down next to her, put my hand on her bare thigh, ate my waffles, and drank my orange juice.

"Mmm, this is so good. Who made this? Shirley?" Jenny asked. "'Cause I know you didn't!"

"My chef made it," I admitted. "But how did you know it wasn't me?"

She snorted. "There isn't a crumb anywhere in this place. You probably don't even make yourself toast!"

We both eyed the toaster oven, which was brand-new, gleaming, and unused.

Jenny turned to me, eyebrow raised. "Need I say more?"

"Ha. No, you don't." I kept my hand on her thigh and finished my waffle. "What would you like to do today, Jenny?"

She shrugged. "I dunno. What do rich people do on a nice day like this?"

"I usually work," I said, "but I'm off." I'd just decided that. We didn't have that much time together, and I intended to enjoy myself.

"Yay!" She grinned at me. "So, what should we do?"

I grabbed her hands. "I think we should go shopping. I want to get you some more dresses if that's okay. I just found out we're invited to the rehearsal dinner tonight at Il Pastorne, which is pretty formal."

Jenny's eyes widened. "You already spent so much on that other dress. You don't have to do that, Cole—"

"I want to do that. If it's okay with you."

She smiled. "Okay," she said, giving in. "That's real nice of you."

"It's my pleasure. Is there anything else you'd like to do?" I asked.

Jenny appeared to take my question seriously. Her pretty face screwed up into a grimace as she went quiet for a minute, considering her choices. "I'd like to go see the seals if that's okay."

I blinked at her. "I'm sorry?"

"The *seals*. You know, the sea animals that are kind of round and look like torpedoes. They have whiskers." She mimed hair coming out of her face.

"I know what a seal is," I assured her, laughing. "I just don't know where we can go see them."

"At the aquarium, silly!" She hopped up and started gathering the dishes. "They have them in a big tank out front. It's free. You can just go there and watch them. I do it all the time."

"You go see the seals all the time...?" This girl was full of surprises.

"Yeah," she said. "They're cute, you know? And I love animals. So sometimes I go stand there and watch them swim."

"That sounds great, Jenny." I hopped up and helped her with the dishes, even though I never picked up after myself. I literally had a "picker-upper," a woman who worked for the management company. She came to the penthouse every day and cleaned up after me when I left for work.

"Yay!" She kissed me on the cheek. "This is going to be the best day *ever*!"

Before we made it out the door, we made love again. Twice. Once in the bed, once in the shower after we'd been in the bed. The second time was by accident—I couldn't seem to keep my hands off Jenny, or my dick out of her for that matter. As soon as she was near me, as soon as my bare skin touched hers, I got hard.

I wasn't exactly complaining about it.

"Your complexion looks real good, Coley," she cooed when we finally made it out the door and into the elevator.

"So does yours." I pulled her against me again for a hot kiss, then released her. "Woah, I need to take it easy. We are not doing it in the elevator."

"Yet," she teased. She looked smug.

Amari was working again. He gave us a broad smile as we crossed the lobby. "Mr. Bryson. Ms. Jenny. It's nice to see you again. It's a lovely day—would you like me to pull the car around?"

"I think we're going to walk. It's about twenty minutes to the aquarium, right?" I asked.

Amari's smile widened. "Yes, it is. Lovely day for a

walk. Enjoy the gorgeous weather, you two." He held the door open for us, and we stepped out into the gorgeous morning.

Boston was not known for its weather, and for good reason. But today was one of those rare days when the sun was shining, and there was no humidity. I held out my hand for Jenny's, vowing to enjoy all my good fortune.

My escort looked beautiful. Her skin and fantastic body were on display in the simple black sundress she'd chosen, which was perfect for the weather. She perched huge sunglasses on her nose and smiled as we walked down the street. "When was the last time you walked to the aquarium?" she asked.

"Never."

"Have you ever been to the aquarium—even when you were a kid?"

"No," I admitted. "My father wasn't one for day trips. And he didn't let our nanny take me out much."

"Oh. You had a nanny?"

"Yep, she was French. Very strict," I said. "But she used to make us macarons, so she wasn't all bad."

"Huh." A note of concern crept into her voice. "And your mom...?"

I shrugged. "She died when I was little."

"I'm so sorry." Jenny sounded like she might cry.

"It's okay." I squeezed her hand. "I don't talk about

her very often, so it makes me happy to think about her. Thank you for asking."

"Aw, that's real nice." She sniffled.

"What about you?" I asked.

"I told you, I go to the aquarium all the time." She squeezed my hand back. "The seals are always there for me. Even when the weather sucks."

Dodging my real question, she didn't say more. Jenny had opened the door by asking about my mom, but she didn't seem as though she was going to walk through it. I had to respect that, even though I wanted to know more about her. But if she wasn't going to offer, I didn't want to pry.

I enjoyed our walk. Even though I was mildly hungover and should have been drained from having all the alcohol and sex possible in the past twenty-four hours, I felt invigorated. Hands linked together, Jenny and I both had a bounce in our step. People we passed on the sidewalk smiled at us. We smiled back. The sun shined down, and the only clouds in the sky were the cute little white puffy ones.

It was like something out of a rom-com, and I didn't watch rom-coms.

Finally, we made it to the aquarium. "There they are!" Jenny pointed to a giant tank located near the entrance.

Massive gray seals covered in black spots swam back and forth, gliding past each other in the clear blue water.

Little children shrieked with delight as they swam past. The exhibit was already crowded, with families milling around, pushing strollers, carrying backpacks, and all the other crap you needed when you had kids. One of the mothers called for her twins, and a space opened up—Jenny hustled me over.

"Look at them! Look at those eyebrows!" The seals had both bushy white whiskers and wiry eyebrows, which they seemed to raise as they swam their laps.

"Aren't they cute?" Jenny cooed. "They remind me of dogs. Big, fat, swimming dogs."

A particularly fat seal somersaulted in front of us, and I laughed. "He's showing off for you."

"That one's named Tuba." Jenny pointed at the chubby guy. "I had to ask one of the girls what his name was—he's such a cutie."

"Tuba? That's funny."

"Yeah, and that one's Reggae and that's Chewbacca…" She rattled off a few more names as the creatures whizzed by.

"You weren't kidding. You really do come here a lot," I said.

Jenny kept her hands on the glass, her eyes on the seals.

She looked genuinely delighted. "They always cheer me up. And it's cheaper than therapy."

I watched as one of the seals floated near Jenny, seeming to wave its flipper. My heart melted a little. "That's true," I agreed.

"Yeah," she said. "And these guys are always here for you. Rain or shine. Good days and bad days. They always make me smile no matter what. How lucky is *that*?"

I turned and inspected Jenny. Her face was so open and happy as the seals torpedoed by, friends that she'd made from her side of the glass.

I'd thought it before, but now I knew for sure. I'd never met anyone like her.

"It's lucky," I agreed again. "Pretty freaking lucky."

CHAPTER 16
Jenny

COLE WASN'T AS OBSESSED WITH THE SEALS AS I was, but he still liked them. After about ten minutes, I was ready to go. "You still want to go shopping?" I asked.

"Do you?"

I shrugged. "Shopping bores me. But you don't," I admitted. "So if you like it, I betcha I can like it."

He smiled at me, and it was like the sun coming out. "Why don't we at least get you dresses for the rehearsal dinner and the wedding, and then we can call it good? I know a place we can go. We can be in and out real quick."

"Are you talking dirty to me, Coley?" I asked.

"Ha." He yanked at the collar of his shirt. "It's automatic, I guess. I can't help myself."

"I don't mind." I linked my hand with his as we crossed the street, heading to Faneuil Hall. "But for the record, you haven't been in and out real quick. Which I appreciate!" I laughed—a loud, honking sound that I could never control. A passing woman in a suit looked at me, startled, but Cole laughed. He didn't seem embarrassed by me. Maybe billionaires were so wealthy they didn't get embarrassed?

"Sorry." I coughed. "I always laugh too loud."

"Don't be sorry." He squeezed my hand. "One of the things I like about you is that you're yourself. So don't apologize."

One of the things he liked about me? Maybe Mr. Billions was having as much fun as I was. Cole did seem to be enjoying himself. When I'd done that thing with his balls in the shower, he shouted. Like, a good shout, something he couldn't control. And then he'd come *hard*. Hot pride bloomed in my chest when I remembered how he'd held on to me for dear life as the orgasm swept through him.

The orgasm he'd had with *me*.

I took pride in my work. I aimed to satisfy my clients, and this assignment was no different. But what was different was that I genuinely wanted to blow Cole's mind. I wanted him to remember me long after these two weeks faded away. I wanted it to mean something.

What exactly I wanted it to mean, I had no idea. But I had a feeling that I wouldn't ever forget about Cole

Bryson, and it would be nice if the billionaire remembered me.

All of this was a fancy way of thinking circles around the fact that I liked my client. I liked holding his hand. I liked his Cayenne Turbo. I liked his glorious penthouse with its view of the Harbor. I also liked his big, long cock.

But underneath that, something was bothering me. It had to do with all the liking going on.

I liked Cole. He was a male version of me, but wicked rich, and sophisticated. So maybe he wasn't that much like me, but whatever! The fact that I genuinely enjoyed my client unnerved me. The fact that I'd had several rocking orgasms with him, which had caused me to scream my head off—for real—troubled me even more. That had never happened to me with a client.

In fact, it had never happened to me *ever*. So why was that? Why did Billionaire Batman have that effect on me?

I glanced at Cole. He wore his sunglasses, his thick, black, wavy hair glinting in the sunlight. His polo shirt strained against his muscular chest, and his brawny forearms bulged with veins. He reeked of money, of class, and of pure testosterone. Who the fuck was this guy? Who the hell did he think he was, stroking my G-spot and making my whole body vibrate like that?

And when could he do it again?

"The store's in Beacon Hill. Do you mind walking some more?" he asked.

"I love it. It's such a gorgeous day." I smiled at the people milling by us, the smell of food wafting out of Faneuil Hall, and the glorious sun shining. Cole and I firmly kept our hands clasped as we navigated through the crowd, past Legal Seafoods, multiple Dunkins, and Downtown Crossing. Holding Cole's hand was the most natural thing in the world. I wasn't pretending to enjoy myself. It felt like he was my actual boyfriend and that maybe I was living a real life.

You are living a real life, said the voice in my head, which was true and not true all at the same time.

Stop confusing me, I ordered. Sometimes, I had to shut that voice up.

Finally, we reached Boston Common. The park was so pretty this time of year. The trees were in full pink bloom, and the grass was a rich green. People watched the swan boats, walked their dogs, and scrolled on their phones as they sat on the park benches. It felt like the whole city was outside. We New Englanders knew how precious this weather was.

We crossed the park into Beacon Hill, a ritzy neighborhood filled with beautiful townhomes and luxury stores. Cole stopped before a boutique with tiny, expensive-looking dresses in the window. I peered inside—the store was sparse and immaculate, and they only sold high-end dresses. It was the kind of place I would never venture into for fear of being so ill-bred and poor I might set off some sort of alarm.

"Here we are." Without a preamble, Cole pulled me inside. It smelled like expensive perfume. A pretty woman stood behind the counter. She had long, raven hair and wore a simple white dress shirt unbuttoned dangerously low.

She smiled at Cole, obviously pleased. "Mr. Bryson, it's always a pleasure," she purred in a sultry, foreign accent. "It's been so long since we've seen you. I've been looking forward to your next visit."

"Hello, Camille." Cole smiled back. "This is my girlfriend, Jenny. She needs dresses for a couple of upcoming events, including a formal wedding."

"Sounds wonderful, Mr. Bryson. Bonjour, Jenny." She eyed me up and down. Apparently, Camille didn't like what she saw because she raised an eyebrow disapprovingly. *"C'est un plaisir."*

"Huh?"

"I said, it's a pleasure." But Camille didn't sound like it was a pleasure. She sounded as if she were talking to a small, very dumb, and annoying child. "It's French. You know, the language?"

"Oh yeah! French *the language*." I nodded as if this was the most profound thing I'd ever heard.

So Camille was French. And I didn't have to speak it to know that (a) she had a thing for Coley and (b) she thought I was a bimbo.

I stuck my chest out at that French bitch and smiled. "Does that gold dress in the window come in a size six?"

"Je suis vraiment désolé." She pursed her lips. "We don't carry anything larger than a four, I'm afraid."

"I'll try the four, then." I tossed my hair over my shoulder. "Sometimes I fluctuate between sizes, and I've been getting plenty of exercise lately." I smacked Cole on the ass for emphasis.

He laughed. She frowned.

I checked my nails while I waited for that bitch to get me the dress.

"Camille, can you actually pull a couple of looks?" Cole asked politely. "We need something for that wedding, too."

"Of course, Mr. Bryson." She still had the sultry accent, but at least she didn't purr at him.

"Like I said, size four should do nicely," I called, sounding anything but nicely. "Working here, being French and speaking French *the language* and all, I'm sure you can find a couple of 'looks' that work!"

"Jenny," Cole said, keeping his voice low while Camille fetched me things to try on, "did Camille offend you?"

"No," I said innocently, "but she *was* eye-fucking you."

Cole shrugged good-naturedly. "I only have eyes for you if that helps."

"It helps," I said. "But also, I think it's rude that they don't carry any sizes bigger than a four. Most girls can't fit their asses into a four, and that's 'cause girls gotta eat. Maybe Camille only eats a croissant once in a full moon, and that's why she's such a bitch. But that's her problem, not mine."

Cole nodded slowly, taking my words in. "Words to live by, Jenny. Words to live by."

I perched my sunglasses on top of my head. "Right? I can't be worrying about everybody else out there. Just trying to keep my side of the street clean, you know what I'm saying?"

Cole kept nodding as Camille hustled back from the changing rooms. "Everything is ready for you, Miss Jenny."

"Thanks a bunch, Camille." I tossed my hair and sashayed past her.

"I'm going to help you screen dresses," Cole offered and followed me back.

He ducked into the changing room behind me and

locked the door. "You can't leave me out there with her alone. She looks *tres* pissed."

"Yeah, well, maybe it'll give old Camille a chance to button her shirt. And take the stick out of her ass."

Cole chuckled as he took a seat on a nearby stool. For such a tiny store, it had a mammoth dressing room. I was still pissed that the salesperson had been judge-y and rude, so I huffed as I stripped out of my clothes and roughly grabbed the first dress. It was pink and ruffled, totally not my style. "Ick, I hate this. Help me zip it."

Cole obeyed, zipping me into the micro mini. He whistled appreciatively. "You might not like that, but you look gorgeous."

"I look like a cheerleading poodle." I frowned at my reflection. "It's a no, Coley. Sorry to disappoint."

"You are anything but disappointing." He chivalrously unzipped the dress and hung it back on the hanger. "How about this one?"

The next dress was a deep purple, pretty but not my style. "Nah."

"This one?" He held up a long, deep-teal, mermaid-looking dress. "This could be nice for the wedding," he encouraged.

"Yeah, all right. I'll try it." I shimmied into the gown while Cole watched. Was I imagining it, or were his eyes getting hooded?

"Zip me, baby, okay?" I cooed in case his arousal wasn't all in my head. I shouldn't let stupid Camille ruin a great day. I was used to women being rude to me—it happened all the time. Either they were jealous, threatened, or snobby. Whatever the reason, they used it to look down on me. Little did they know it wasn't all fun and games being so young and hot. I mean, it could have been, in an alternate universe, but that was not the universe I was living in.

"Ooh, I like this one." I smiled at myself in the mirror. The formal dress clung to me but was so expensive it still looked classy. "I might wear my hair up with this." I pulled my curls up into a messy bun and made a kissy face at Cole in the mirror.

"You look stunning." Before I knew what hit me, he was off the stool and behind me. But after a second, I knew *exactly* what was hitting me!

"Mmm, you're so beautiful, Jenny. And feisty. I love it when you show your claws a little." He ran his mouth down my neck, causing goose bumps everywhere.

"Cole, what are you doing?"

"This." He unzipped the mermaid gown and gently hung it up.

Then he pressed his screaming erection against my ass, and it was game on!

"You're so naughty, baby." I rubbed up against him, and he moaned. "But we can't do it in public."

"We're not in public." Cole stripped out of his shirt and unbuttoned his pants so they fell down around his ankles. "We're in a dressing room—totally different, babe. And I can't wait. I need you."

"Well, when you put it that way…" I pushed down his boxer briefs, and his glorious cock sprang out at me, fully erect and at attention. My insides got all squirmy. We didn't have long—Camille could come back and check on us any second.

I hitched my thong to the side and rubbed my already wet slit against him.

"Oh fuck, babe," he panted. "You're so wet."

He thrust against my slit, hitting my swollen clit, and I cried out.

"I need to be inside you. I'm not gonna last long."

"S'okay, Coley," I cooed. "I like it when you give it to me hard."

He picked me up. I wrapped my legs around him, laughing, as he pinned me against the wall.

But then he entered me, hard and deep, and I wasn't laughing anymore.

I was flying.

Cole thrust his muscular hips, driving into me. I didn't know if his penis had some sort of a curve or was just magic, but it stroked that spot deep inside me that no one had ever reached. "Oh yeah. That's it, babe. Just like that." The words flew out of my mouth, loud and uninhibited, before I could stop them.

"Fuck, yeah. I'm gonna give it to you, Jenny. Oh my fucking God, you're unbelievable." His thrusts became rougher, a look of pure ecstasy on his face. I reached down and stroked his balls like I'd done in the shower, and he cried out. *Loud*.

I slapped one hand over his mouth but didn't stop stroking with the other. His balls tightened underneath my touch, and pure female satisfaction surged through me. He was going to come. He was going to come for *me*.

I bounced up and down on his long, hard cock, my climax building deep inside me.

"Fuck!" Cole screamed against my palm as he came. Feeling his hot seed inside me pushed my orgasm over the edge. My eyes rolled back in my head as I flew higher and higher, my body vibrating with magic Cole-Bryson penis delight.

Cole slapped his hand over my mouth as I cried out, but I didn't even notice.

When I returned to earth, I realized we had our hands over each other's mouths.

We both burst out laughing, but you couldn't really hear it.

"Mr. Bryson? Ms. Jenny? Do you need another gown?" Camille sniffed from outside the dressing room.

I took my hand off Cole's mouth. "Nah, we're good," he called. "We'll take all of these!"

And then we burst out laughing again.

CHAPTER 17
Cole

BETWEEN THE SEALS, THE SHOPPING, AND ALL THE sex, I'd seriously been neglecting my phone. There were five messages from Shirley, which I answered. The *Forbes* photo shoot had gone well. She asked me how Jenny was, and I responded with a single thumbs-up emoji, which I hoped would quell her appetite for information.

Probably not, but it was worth a shot.

There were also messages from Kevin that my father still hadn't received the approvals from Ramos and was getting more agitated by the minute. I didn't respond. I felt sorry for Kevin, but he could at least quit my father and walk away.

It wasn't as easy for me, his only son.

Jenny chose the gold-lamé dress for the rehearsal

dinner. It was short and showcased her unforgettable legs. I wondered if we could manage sex in the elevator on the way down, but I forced myself to behave. If the Windsor sisters caught us doing *that*, I might actually get evicted.

Il Pastorne was one of the fanciest restaurants in Boston. It was a short walk from the Liberty, although with Jenny's spiked heels, it still took us a few minutes to get there. She let out a whistle when we reached the building. It was white, old-fashioned, and proper, much like the Prestons themselves.

"This is even fancier than the last place!" She blinked up at the white-stone facade.

"It's stupid-fancy, but the food's *ah*-mazing." I preferred a more casual atmosphere, like Alfonso's, but even I had to admit that the food at Il Pastorne was second to none. "You'll love it."

"Just don't order me any of that grilled octopus stuff, Coley," she warned. "Or you won't be getting any action tonight!"

I laughed. "I don't know if I can handle any more action tonight," I admitted. We'd had sex in the shower *again* when we returned to the penthouse that afternoon. "But I promise I won't order octopus."

"Good thing, baby." She positioned herself at my side as we prepared to enter the restaurant.

"You look beautiful, Jenny. That dress is the bomb."

She smiled up at me and tossed her hair. "I have a very special billionaire to thank for it. Now stop lookin' at me like that, or we'll get arrested for indecent exposure or something."

We headed inside, and I took a deep breath. Il Pastorne's interior was gorgeous, pristine, and formal, with crystal chandeliers, soaring ceilings, and white tablecloths. Jenny looked impressed with the surroundings, ogling all the crystal and tuxedoed waitstaff. I felt like I was seeing the restaurant for the first time through her eyes. It made me appreciate it more.

Still, part of me wanted to throw her over my shoulder, carry her back to the penthouse, lay in bed, and watch New England Sports Network till we fell asleep. James and I had been friends forever, but his family was not my favorite. His brother Todd was okay. But his father was uptight, silent, and vaguely disapproving, and his mother was an absolute stone-cold bitch. Celia Preston liked me and approved of my friendship with James, but that's because I had a trust fund and a pedigree. My father belonged to the country club and had a second home on Nantucket; the Bryson family was of use to Celia Preston. We passed the test.

Audrey had nothing to offer them—no connections, fortune, or fabulous second home that could be borrowed to host a fundraising gala. Celia would never approve of her. And if she found out she was a professional escort? She'd absolutely lose her shit.

I glanced at Jenny, wondering for the first time what my father would think of the fact that I'd hired an escort. *Who cares?* I didn't, but I also had a feeling he would be angry. Nothing was more important than his name, his business, his legacy.

Good thing what I did was none of his business.

"There they are." Jenny pointed at James and Audrey.

They were both dressed up and looked great. It did not escape my notice that they also looked every inch a real couple.

"Dre!" Jenny whooped, racing to give Audrey a jiggly hug. "This place is frickin' amazing!"

Audrey smiled at her, but the smile seemed laced with worry. "It's gorgeous. Just like you—you're looking really good, Jenny."

Jenny tossed her curls and modeled her gold-lamé dress. "Coley bought it for me."

"Coley?" James asked, raising his eyebrows at me. "For real?"

I punched him on the shoulder. "For real, bro. So shut up."

James dragged me to the long table where his entire family was seated, along with Evie's family, all sorts of cousins, and friends. James's father sat at the head of the table, resplendent in a custom-made suit. Celia Preston sat beside him, eyeing the guests over her martini. In particular, her gaze returned repeatedly to Audrey.

I wasn't the only one who'd noticed they looked like a real couple.

James sat Audrey with Jenny and me at one end of the table. He joined Todd and Evie, who looked happy and excited. James grabbed a glass of champagne from a passing waiter and raised it.

"I'd like to make a toast," he said. All eyes turned to him except for Celia Preston, who was now watching Audrey and Jenny with a thinly veiled look of distaste on her face. But Audrey was watching James, a smile on her face that looked real. She nodded at him in encouragement.

"My baby brother is all grown up," James said, patting Todd on the shoulder. "And I'm happy to announce he's marrying the woman that he loves. Evie, I know that you love my brother. I do. Seeing you two together for the past week has been inspiring. I expect good things for you in the future."

Celia Preston tore her gaze away from the girls and watched her older son. She looked shocked—James was rarely so cheerful. She was probably waiting for the other shoe to drop.

"So I'd like to toast the happy couple. Cheers to your

wedding tomorrow and for a lifetime of happiness to follow." Everyone cheered, and James leaned down to Todd and whispered something. They both looked like they were tearing up.

What planet was I on? James Preston was not an emotional guy.

But whatever he said must've got the happy couple going—Todd and Evie started making out at the table. Celia Preston almost spit out her martini.

Then James sat down next to Audrey and pulled her in for a long, lingering kiss, and Celia Preston almost choked.

I laughed and threw my arm around Jenny, relieved that I did not ever have to deal with any of this shit.

AFTER DINNER—MORE importantly, after I watched James fawning all over Audrey at dinner—the girls went to the ladies' room. I dragged James to the bar. "Dude," I said. I ordered two bourbons.

"Yes, dude?" James asked. "Actually—aren't we too old for that now? We used to say that at Wharton. It makes me sad to hear it come out of my mouth now. It's like I'm an old-timer."

"An old-timer who's ready to settle down?" I asked.

James narrowed his eyes at me. "Do you have to go there tonight, *Coley*?"

"Fuck you," I said good-naturedly. I sipped my bourbon. "You know you've got an emotional boner for that girl on your forehead though, right?"

"An emotional boner? I didn't know they existed."

"It's like a heart on your sleeve, but bigger and more obnoxious." I laughed. "And you totally have one."

"She offered me a crab cake today, and I didn't eat it," he objected.

"You've fucked her, though. I can tell. Like, fifty times this week I bet," I said.

He shrugged. "Not fifty."

I puffed my chest out. "Then Jenny and I are winning."

"Haven't you been to work?" James asked me. He sounded simultaneously disgusted and impressed.

"Nah—I took the day off." I shrugged. "This girl is like a drug for me. I can't keep my dick out of her."

James arched his eyebrow. "Does that qualify as an emotional boner? Or are you two just sort of disgusting?"

"I don't know," I admitted. "I seriously can't keep my hands off her. Is that...*love*?" I hadn't even considered it.

"It sounds sort of like it. But it could just be lust," James said.

"There's definitely lust," I said.

"Do you *like* her?"

"I'm fucking crazy about her," I said, the words springing out. *Oh fuck. Did I just say that out loud?*

James looked at me. I looked at him. Then he patted me on the shoulder as if he were consoling me.

Audrey and Jenny were headed back toward us, both of them laughing. Audrey looked happy, Jenny looked delighted, and they both looked gorgeous.

"Dude," I chided. It was my turn to console him! "Put your emotional boner away. It's embarrassing."

But as the girls reached us, I felt relieved. I put my arm around Jenny, my palm sliding down to cradle her ass. It felt like my hand belonged there. It felt like it was *meant to be* there.

Which left me wondering. Did I actually have an emotional boner, too?

And if I did...what the hell was I going to do about it?

CHAPTER 18
Jenny

AUDREY HAULED ME TO THE BATHROOM AFTER dinner. We headed to the other end of the restaurant to avoid James's family and anyone else connected to the wedding.

"Why're you dragging me out to Timbuktu?" I asked.

"I want to know how things are going with Mr. Billions," she said.

"Well, I want to know what's going on with *your* Mr. Billions. Tell me everything!"

Audrey shook her head. "I like him," she admitted. "But I know it's not going anywhere."

"Aw, c'mon Dre. Why're you still talking like that?" I asked. "I saw you two out there. You are on The Love Boat."

"It's not like that, Jenny. I'm not right for him."

"Says who?" I argued.

"Says me. It's complicated." She sighed. She glanced over her shoulder, making sure that no one was around. "James finally opened up to me a little. He told me that he'd had a girlfriend when he was younger—her name was Danielle, and she was really smart. She was supposed to go to an Ivy League school and everything. But his mother didn't like her."

She lowered her voice further and continued, "I guess they got into a big fight one night with his parents. After Danielle left, she got into a car accident and died. His mother told him he was lucky—that he dodged a bullet."

"Dre! That's awful. His mother's the devil, huh?" I looked over my shoulder, too, just in case. I guess there was a reason Audrey was dragging my ass to Timbuktu. Celia Preston was a stone-cold bitch!

"She's obsessed with their status and reputation." Audrey grimaced. "And if Danielle wasn't good enough for James, you know I'm not. But anyway, it's too depressing to think about. Can you distract me?"

I linked my arm through hers. "I can try."

Audrey's expression softened. "Tell me what's going on with you and Cole, okay? Bonus points if you can cheer me up."

"I'll do what I can—but I'm sorry that James's mom is evil." I squeezed my friend's arm.

"Thanks, Jenny." She smiled at me. "I appreciate it. But there's nothing I can do—honestly, I don't want to think about it anymore. So please tell me how things are going with Cole."

"It's been pretty busy. I mean, we've been *getting* pretty busy." I laughed, my honking sound carrying down the hall. I needed to cheer poor Dre up, so I should dish. "We even did it in the dressing room at a snotty French boutique!"

Her jaw dropped. "Tell me everything."

We headed into the private bathroom, setting ourselves up by the well-lit vanity. Il Pastorne's bathroom antechamber was nice enough to move into and pay rent. I pulled my makeup bag out of my purse.

"Cole's frickin' crazy!" I applied more blush and lip gloss, then fluffed my hair. "I swear to God, I've never been with someone who wants to have this much sex. He can't keep his hands off me."

"Even in the dressing room at a fancy store?" Audrey asked.

"Yeah. He totally thinks he's above the law, right? It's a billionaire thing—he thinks the rules don't apply to him.

"He just followed me when I was trying this dress on. We weren't in there for two seconds, and he pinned me up against the wall. With the sales-clerk right outside! He had to lift me up so she couldn't see our feet together. And he fucked me like crazy. I had to slap my hand over his mouth though 'cause he's a yeller when he comes. Real loud, Dre. Real loud. And he likes me to do this thing with his balls—"

"Jenny—I didn't mean it! Don't actually tell me *everything*." Audrey clapped her hands over her ears. "I don't need to know the thing about his balls!"

I fanned myself. "Fine. But I'm gettin' hot just thinking about it. I should be exhausted, but I'm not. Jesus. He's worse than Loopsy and Fat Vinnie put together."

My friend blinked at me. "Do you *like* him?"

"Are you kidding me? This is the best time I've had with a John *ever*. It's like we're the same person. Except he's rich, and he's a guy. And that thing with his balls."

"Huh," she said.

"Huh is right." I turned and inspected my friend's face. Enough about me. Audrey and James had been all over each other again tonight. They seemed like a real couple. I'd seen the way James was looking at my friend. She might be his hired date, but he had real feelings for her. I could tell.

"Mr. Sex in a Suit is a little romance-y tonight, Dre. He's got it real bad. I almost feel sorry for him," I said. "Did you bat him around like a cat toy last night?"

"I might have... a little." Audrey pursed her lips.

I nodded at her. "It worked. You better watch it. I know that look he's got."

"Jenny, stop."

She paused and then said, "What look is that, exactly?"

I rolled my eyes. "I think he might be in love with you. I'm just sayin'." I shrugged. "He doesn't look like he's pretending anymore."

"That only happens in the movies."

"Then I'll come over and film you," I snapped. "Jesus, Dre. You gotta loosen up a little. Sometimes good things happen to good people."

"Huh," she said again.

"Huh is right. Let's go. We don't want your Mr. Suit to cry because he misses you… and Coley's hand hasn't been on my ass in more than five minutes. My butt's gettin' cold."

I nodded at her as we left. "And James's mother is the devil, but that doesn't mean things can't work out with you guys. You just might wanna skip the holidays!"

"Fair enough, Jenny." Audrey laughed and shook her head. "Fair enough."

THE REHEARSAL DINNER WAS FUN. We drank a ton of wine. We ate delicious food, including tiramisu, and nobody tried to feed me a seared octopus. Cole and I hung out with Audrey and James, talking, laughing, and acting as if we were on the best double date ever. Which we were. Except that Dre and I were escorts, and all of this was just for show.

But at some point, my show had crossed the line into reality TV. When I laughed at Cole's jokes, I wasn't faking. They were funny. When I kissed him and snuggled against him, it felt good. It felt good in my heart, where I had no business feeling anything. I watched Audrey, knowing that she felt the same way about James. She had real feelings for him. I was screwed; I knew that. But I still held out hope for my good-girl friend. I prayed she would get a happily ever after out of this.

I knew better than to hope that for myself.

It was getting late. Cole and I made our final rounds, saying good night. We stopped to pose for a picture with Todd and Evie.

"Everybody get together and smile," the photographer said.

When he finished, Todd turned to us. "We'd love to have you guys join us for the honeymoon," he said. Evie stood at his side, nodding vigorously.

"We just think having you there will be more fun," she added. "The resort we're staying at is gorgeous. Right on the water, and it's supposed to be the best beach in the world. Everything is five-star, and everyone's coming. Todd's parents, my parents, my cousins, James and Audrey..." She put her hands together, begging. "We want this to be a celebration and the trip of a lifetime. You guys will liven things up!"

Cole turned to me. "Do you want to go to the Caribbean, babe?"

I squeezed his hand so hard it probably hurt. This was what I'd been hoping for. "Are you freakin' kidding me? Of course, I want to go to the Caribbean! White sand beaches and fruity drinks with little umbrellas in them? I live for that shit!"

"It appears we're a yes," Cole said, laughing. "Thank you for the invite. We'll see you guys tomorrow. Congratulations."

"Yay!'" Evie said. She pulled Todd in for another hot kiss. The happy couple hadn't been able to keep their hands off each other all night, which made me dislike her less. She'd been too preoccupied to thrust her chest out at my man. My fake date. My John. Whatever!

The photographer snapped a few more pictures. Then Cole steered me toward the exit. "You're adorable, babe."

"I'm a little excited. I've never been to an island before," I admitted. "I hope it's okay that I want to go."

"Oh, it's more than okay." He secured his hand firmly on my ass as we headed back toward the Liberty. "I haven't taken a vacation in a while. We're going to have a blast."

I nestled against him. I was tired and grateful for his big body next to mine. "I had fun tonight. Evie's not all bad, I guess. It was nice that she invited us on their vacation."

"Of course, she invited us. Her cousins think I'm eye candy." Cole laughed. "Wait till they see you in a thong bikini—that's *real* eye candy!"

I yawned. "I don't think James's mother will approve."

"She doesn't approve of much."

"I know...she seems real cold. Like she has an icicle shoved up her ass. I don't think she likes me or Audrey too much." I wrinkled my nose. "And it doesn't matter if she likes me, but Dre's another story. She should give her a chance."

"Celia Preston isn't one for giving chances." He frowned. "I keep meaning to ask you. why do you call Audrey 'Dre'?"

"It's a nickname." I shrugged. "When she started at the agency, she thought 'Audrey' sounded too prim and proper. We were trying to make her name have more pop to it." I snapped my fingers.

"She looks like an Audrey to me," Cole said.

"Yeah, I know. But she'll always be my Dre. She's my best friend, you know?"

"It's nice that you two have each other." But his brow furrowed.

"It is nice," I said. "So why do you look all dark and stormy?"

"I guess I don't like thinking about why it's nice." A deep V formed between his eyebrows, and he pulled me closer.

"So don't think about it." I gave him a playful nudge. "And stop scowling, or you're going to need Botox!"

Cole laughed, and we walked arm in arm to the Liberty. I didn't want him getting upset thinking about me and Dre back at AccommoDating. I didn't want to face it, either. I liked being with Cole. I liked Audrey being with James. I enjoyed our happy little bubble and didn't want to think about what came after.

Because what came after was going to suck compared to this.

We stumbled into the lobby, laughing and talking, only to stop dead in our tracks. The Windsor sisters were waiting for the elevator. They did a double take when they saw us, then shot each other a pointed look.

"Here we go," Cole said under his breath. "A drunken duel in the Liberty lobby. You ready, babe?"

I nodded. I'd had precisely enough alcohol to be primed to fight. "What are we dueling about, again?"

"Eh..." Cole shrugged.

The last time we'd seen the sisters, we'd told them they were rude. Or they told us *we* were rude? After so many glasses of wine, I couldn't really remember. But I did remember them telling Cole they would try to get him kicked out of the building.

"Oh, *hello*," Greta Windsor said, voice icy. "I'm surprised to see you, Cole."

She lowered her trendy eyeglasses, all the better to look down on us. "I guess you haven't received your eviction notice yet."

Cole snorted. "Have you gotten yours?"

"No," she sniffed, "and I don't expect to. But then again, I'm not the one breaking the law and violating the co-op regulations. *You* are."

Cole arched his eyebrow. "Exactly how many Manhattans did you drink tonight, Greta? You're drunk. Time to go night-night!"

"Har de har har. I'm not drunk, Cole. At least, not drunk enough to be mistaken about *you*." She smiled at him, the cat who relished its torture of the canary. "You've broken the law, and you can't break the law and be an owner here. As I said, the Liberty is for upstanding citizens with flawless pedigrees. Not for people like you. So you won't be living here much longer, I'm afraid."

Florence cleared her throat, her cue to pipe in. "It's too bad that we won't have to listen to your endless late-night rooftop parties or tolerate your...um...*friends*."

She eyed me up and down. "We'll be returning to a higher-caliber clientele around here, just as the building was intended. We have to keep the riffraff out, you know? Otherwise, property values will plummet."

"First of all, do not speak to Jenny like that." Cole took a menacing step forward, and the sisters instinctively stepped back.

"Second of all, you are both talking out of your white, wrinkled asses," he said. "I haven't broken any laws. Unless you mean some global warming violation?" He grabbed my hand and pulled me next to him. "Jenny and I *are* raising the temperature around here because we're so hot." He managed to look cocky and menacing all simultaneously, God bless him.

That made me laugh. The large, honking sound startled Florence and Greta, which suited me fine.

Cole pulled me closer and gave them a death stare. "As the saying goes, if you can't take the heat, move the hell out. If anyone's getting evicted, it's you two."

Greta lifted her chin. "We aren't talking about any

global-warming nonsense, and *we* are certainly not getting evicted. We haven't broken any laws—but you have."

The elevator dinged, and they climbed inside as if daring us to join them. We did not.

"We know all about Jenny, you see. Your 'girlfriend' is an illegal sex worker. We have all the proof we need, so we're reporting you to the authorities." Greta looked triumphant. "So bye-bye, Bryson."

My stomach sank, but Cole took her accusation in stride. "Bye-bye, Greta. And Florence," he said. "Good luck taking the sticks out of your asses tonight. Better you than me with that job—they're jammed in there pretty tight." He smirked as the doors closed.

But as soon as we were alone in the lobby, he cursed. "Fuck! How did they find out about you?"

"I dunno, Coley." But I got on my phone and started scrolling. Lo and behold, there were already pictures of us online, most of them from the previous party. I hadn't worried about it, because we'd been having so much fun. But there had been photographers at all the events, and Cole and I had posed for multiple shots.

I showed him a picture of us from the *Herald*'s gossip column. We were smiling, Cole's arm thrown around me: *Boston mogul Cole Bryson and his date.*

"They don't even have your name in there," Cole said. "How the heck did the Windsors track you?"

"Like you said, they're wicked rich. And bored. They probably hired somebody to dig me up on the Internet and *boom*. They linked me back to the agency." My shoulders slumped. "I'm real sorry. I hope you don't get evicted 'cause of me."

"I'm not getting evicted, and you don't have to apologize. You didn't do anything wrong." But his face had that dark and stormy look again.

"I'm still sorry." I tentatively reached over and held his hand.

He didn't pull away from me, which was a good thing.

But I didn't know how long I had before that happened. If his nosy neighbors knew I was a hooker, the news could spread and fast. Cole might think it wasn't a big deal, but I knew how this worked. He was worth billions. I was worth less than nothing. Billionaires and call-girls did not compute, not in any math I ever saw.

I felt like Cinderella when her chariot turned back into a pumpkin and all the pretty horses returned to being mice. It was only a matter of time before it turned to midnight, and the full spell was broken.

And what the hell was I going to do after that?

CHAPTER 19
Cole

THE WINDSOR SISTERS DIDN'T SCARE ME. AS FAR as I was concerned, they could go die in a hole. They had money, but I had more money. They had time on their hands and an axe to grind, but I had all the best lawyers and all the best everyone else. I could bury them. I *would* bury them now that they'd gone and pissed me off. I didn't like how they'd spoken to Jenny. They were going to pay dearly for their transgression.

No, the Windsors weren't my concern. But if they could find out about Jenny so quickly, so could other people. And therein lay the problem.

While Jenny washed off her makeup, I checked my phone. And there, just as suspected, were several more text messages from Kevin, my father's assistant. These were ones I couldn't ignore.

> Me again. He asked me to send this:

There was a picture of me and Jenny from the party.

> He wants to know who the girl is. Between you and me, he already has someone looking into her.

> Thanks for the heads-up. I'll deal with it.

Sighing, I turned my phone off. This was what I'd been worried about. If Florence and Greta found out about Jenny, so could my father. And he was way worse than my nosy neighbors.

I stared out at the night sky, thoughts racing. My "girlfriend" was a hooker. So what? What would he do with this information? Would Daddy call the police on me? I doubted it. He needed my professional connections. On top of that, AccommoDating's Madam had assured me that their business was perfectly legal—on paper. So, what did I have to worry about? His approval? My father hadn't seemed to approve of me for a long time...

Florence and Greta Windsor wanted to get me evicted. That was straightforward and, therefore, easy to combat. But my father... He was a hell of a lot trickier than my douche-y neighbors. I'd been fighting him for years and still hadn't figured him out.

I didn't say a word to Jenny as she climbed into bed and snuggled beside me. What was the point? I didn't want to make her upset. It wasn't her fault that the Internet existed. It wasn't her fault that people on message boards talked and that if you looked hard enough, you could probably find out anything about anybody.

It wasn't her fault I'd hired her.

"Good night. Thanks for another great day." She nestled against my chest.

"Thank you." I kissed the top of her head.

"Are you tired...?" She yawned but tried to hide it.

"Hell yes, I'm tired. We had sex, like, six hundred times today." I laughed. "Go to sleep."

"Okay, Coley. Good night." Jenny stilled and fell asleep almost immediately, lightly snoring. She took up more than her side of the bed. Far from annoying, I found it charming as she burrowed deeper under the covers and against my side.

Warm protectiveness surged through me. Poor Jenny. The Windsors were such bitches. *"We have to keep the riffraff out, you know?"* What the hell did Greta or Florence know about anything? Jenny still hadn't told me about her life, but it didn't take much imagination to figure out. It probably hadn't been too cushy.

My neighbors pissed me off; my father exhausted me.

Part of me wanted to ignore his inquiry, ignore *him*. I was my own man. I made my own money, and I had my own life. It didn't matter to me that I'd paid for a fake girlfriend. In many ways, it was the best money I'd ever spent.

But another part of me knew that my father would use any leverage he could to his advantage. It was only a matter of time. Dodging his inquiry wouldn't make him go away —he only got more demanding when ignored.

Unease settled over me as I fell into a restless sleep. For once, I seemed to have more problems than the Thunder's crappy defensive lineup. That wasn't how I liked things. I'd built my world so that I was always in control. I was the boss, the dealmaker, the giver and taker-away-er of good fortune.

So why did I feel like things were getting away from me somehow?

After tossing and turning, I rolled over and looked at the clock: three a.m. Ugh. I threw my arm around Jenny, holding her warm body beside mine. I only had her for a little while. I should enjoy our time together. Still, something nagged at me. I couldn't fall back asleep; I wasn't at ease.

"I'm fucking crazy about her." Those words had slipped out of my mouth and into my best friend's ear, and they were the truth. I was crazy about Jenny. I couldn't

keep my hands off her. If we were near each other, my arm was around her. The sex was incredible and had been from the first go. But more importantly, I genuinely liked her.

I put my face against her skin and inhaled her coconut scent. Why did she smell so good? I didn't know. I just knew I wanted to hold her body next to mine and just… keep holding it.

I had no idea what to do with that information. I'd never stopped running away from women long enough to like one of them. And I didn't even know if she liked me back.

Jenny seemed to enjoy spending time with me. But then again, I was paying her a small fortune to act like she was into me. Maybe she was a great actress, but I felt a real connection between us. In the scheme of things, what did that mean?

I was a billionaire who valued my freedom. She was an escort. People like us didn't exactly live "normal" lives that involved 2.5 kids and a house in the suburbs.

Maybe I could buy her a condo, I mused. Possibly, Jenny could be my "kept woman," or whatever they used to call it. I could send Shirley out to buy her groceries twice a week and sleep over on the weekends. Jenny wouldn't have to work at the agency anymore. She could just sit in her condo and…sit in her condo.

I filed away the confusion swirling in my brain, vowing to ponder it another day. Like never.

And then, in typical-me fashion, I distracted myself by thinking of hockey plays until I finally fell asleep.

CHAPTER 20
Cole

THE MORNING OF THE WEDDING DAWNED. IT WAS another sunny and lovely day, prolonging an almost unheard-of streak of nice weather in Boston. While Jenny was still asleep, I turned my phone back on. There were five messages from Kevin and one from Shirley.

I opened the one from Shirley first.

> The Forbes shoot went well. Do you need me to do any more shopping?

Even though it was six a.m., I called her. "Jenny and I are going to the Caribbean tomorrow with the wedding party."

"Oh, Mr. Bryson—that's wonderful news!" Shirley sounded alert and fully caffeinated. I could picture her, already dressed for the day, entirely made up and ready to go. "Did you have fun at the party? I saw some of the pictures online. Jenny looked so pretty in that dress—"

"Yes, thank you," I interrupted. "Can you shop for some resort wear for her? And bikinis. I want lots of bikinis. Thong bikinis."

"Yes, Mr. Bryson!" Shirley said gleefully. "I'll get right on it!"

"And what about the other thing? The present?" I'd almost forgotten I'd asked Shirley to pick up something else for Jenny.

"Oooh, I got it!" She sounded beside herself with excitement. "Amari had your picker-upper put the gift in your dresser. It's all wrapped and everything!"

"Thanks, Shirley. You're the best."

"Thank *you*, Mr. Bryson. Have a great day!" She hung up on me faster than she ever had before, probably eager to begin her next round of Jenny-related shopping.

I poured myself a cup of coffee before I read Kevin's texts.

> Your father already called me this morning

> He said he knows about the girl. He didn't say more, but that you'd know what he meant

> He asked if you could meet him at the club for breakfast

> He knows the wedding is today
>
> But apparently, he doesn't care

Fuck. Kevin must've been stressed. He rarely texted without punctuation.

> I'll head to the club.
>
> Leaving now. Tell him to wait.
>
> Then take a break, Kev. I'm sure you need one.

It did occur to me after I put my phone down that I'd similarly abused Shirley that morning. Like my father, I'd texted my assistant at the crack of dawn. At least Shirley seemed excited about going shopping again.

You're not your father, said the voice in my head.

FFS, I hoped not.

I scrawled out a quick note to Jenny.

> *Good Morning!*
> *Happy Todd-and-Evie wedding day.*
> *I have a quick business meeting. Be right back.*
> *Chef left breakfast in the fridge, and please help yourself to coffee.*
> *Can't wait to see you in that dress, babe.*

xx,
Cole

The thing was, I *couldn't* wait to see Jenny in the pretty gown we'd bought at the boutique. I had fond memories of that shopping trip! I couldn't remember ever being genuinely invested in what one of my dates wore. But we'd picked the mermaid dress out together. I was uncharacteristically excited about going to the wedding and the reception—if I could just get through the meeting with my father first.

I reached the Liberty's bright, polished lobby, the harbor sparkling outside. The Windsor sisters were nowhere to be seen, but faithful Amari was at the front desk. "Do you ever sleep?" I asked him.

Amari smiled, but he looked uncomfortable. "Ha, I do. Sometimes. Listen, Mr. Bryson—"

"I know all about what Greta and Florence are up to." I waved my hand.

"Yeah, they filed some sort of petition with the boss. And then they bent my ear all about it. I'm sorry—I didn't want to listen to their garbage about Ms. Jenny. But it's hard to walk away from one of the tenants. I have to be polite, you know?" Amari asked.

"You have nothing to apologize for," I assured him. "I

know what they're like. They shouldn't have put you in that position."

He shook his head. "All they do is complain. You think maybe they could just enjoy all that money they've got instead."

"Some people thrive on being miserable, and misery loves company." I shrugged. "Have John call me if he's concerned. Actually—call him. Tell him I'd like to buy out the Windsors' unit. I'll pay double what it's worth, cash, and I'm ready to close whenever he is. Tell him to write me up a Purchase and Sales Agreement, and we're good to go."

Amari's jaw dropped. I was, after all, talking about a six-million-dollar cash deal. He managed to nod his head. "Y-Yes, sir."

"We haven't got time for their shit, am I right? I'm handling it, Amari. I should've done this months ago." I patted him on the back and headed outside.

Why hadn't I thought of buying out those bitches before? Jenny was like my good luck charm. She was helping me turn things around. Now, only if she could help me with the Thunder's defense, and also, my father…

His club, The Bromfield, was located in the Financial District and was a short walk from the Liberty. It was the oldest racquetball and squash club in the city. It boasted a lap pool, sauna, and a dining room filled with solid oak tables, oil paintings of hunting dogs, and red leather chairs. The restaurant had chicken liver pate, green peas, and even turnips on the menu. It was about as old-school as you could get.

Although it was ridiculously expensive, I was also a member, but I never went. I paid my dues mostly to annoy my father. If he could afford it, so could I—I just liked to remind him of that.

The young, besuited attendant rolled his eyes when I reached the entrance. "Dude, you know I'm not supposed to let you in when you're wearing sweats."

"Dude, deal with it." I slapped five hundred dollars into his hand and patted him on the back. "If they threaten to fire you, tell them I'll pull my funding for the fundraiser next month."

"Yes, Mr. Bryson," he groaned.

I found my father in the stately dining room at a table by himself, eating oatmeal with what looked like apricot preserves on top. *Ick.* His hair was wet around the edges. He had probably already worked out, taken a shower, and had plenty of coffee, all the better to chew me a new asshole for dating an escort.

He blinked at me as I sat down. "How did you get in here dressed like that?"

I glanced down at my hoodie and sweats. "These are Lanvin," I said as if the designer label explained everything.

He sighed. "You're supposed to wear a collared shirt here. There's a dress code."

"I know, Father. I've been coming here since I was a little kid. And I'm a member, remember?"

"Then you should know better." He ate some more of his preserves before speaking again. "I saw your pictures online."

I braced myself. "Yes, Father?"

"It's come to my attention that your new lady-friend is... How do I say this?" he asked. "That she's less than legitimate."

"She's legitimately my lady-friend," I said.

He dabbed his mouth with his napkin and frowned. "She's an escort. She works for an agency in the South End. I know all about them."

I raised my eyebrows. I didn't want to ask how he knew about AccommoDating.

He shook his head as if he anticipated my train of thought. "Nothing like that, son. But I do have some colleagues who've used the agency before. Enough about that—the point is, you can't be linked to a prostitute. If it gets out, it'll be a scandal. And scandals are fine except when you're in the real estate business because, in real estate, it's—"

"All about the relationship. I know, I know." I motioned to a passing waiter, and he brought me a coffee.

"But I'm not worried about a scandal, Father. You might be. But I'm not."

My father took a deep breath. For the first time, I noticed that he had dark circles under his eyes. He looked tired.

"You'll care about a scandal if it gets in the way of your inheritance. I know how cocky you are, trust me." He sat back in his chair. "But what if I told you that if you don't break it off with this girl and bury the story, you won't get my empire when I die?"

I blinked at him. Part of the reason I'd built my immense wealth was to inoculate myself from a threat like this. I didn't need his money. I had plenty of my own. Still, I was an only child. There was nobody else but me. "Who are you going to leave it to, Dad?"

He smiled at me, and it wasn't a nice smile.

"Remember that coach you fired last month?"

I shook my head, confused. Since when did my father pay attention to the Thunder's staffing changes? "Yeah... Of course, I do. Because I fired him last month."

"I'm going to give *him* all the money. And maybe to the two lousy neighbors that're trying to get you evicted."

"The Windsor sister? And Todd, the hockey coach?" I could barely remember the guy's last name. He'd only worked for me for a little while.

Dad's smile was now a gloat. "Yes and yes. Further, I'm

going to track down every person you've ever disliked in your life, and I'm going to give them the money. It's not like I've got anything better to do. Ramos still hasn't given me those approvals," he said bitterly.

"You're serious about this?" For so long, my father had only elicited a vague response from me, a yearning to avoid him. But now I was stunned. "You're going to name my enemies as beneficiaries in your will?"

"You know, Cole, your mother would be so upset if she could see you now." A flush crept up the old man's cheeks. "She raised you to be a good person. But all you've done is squander your life. Yeah, you've made money. But you've got no family, no kids. Never even brought a girl home for Christmas. And now you're dating a prostitute." He practically spit the word out. "I expected more from you."

"Yeah, well." I rose to go. "That makes two of us, Dad."

"Don't you walk out on me," he called, his voice menacing.

But I did walk out, and I didn't stop. My father could threaten me all he wanted, but it didn't matter. He was dead to me.

And I wasn't afraid of ghosts.

CHAPTER 21
Jenny

COLE WAS GONE WHEN I GOT UP. I READ HIS note, which was cute. I was also looking forward to the wedding and wearing the dress he'd picked. Todd and Evie were in love. Today was their special day, and then we were all going to the *Caribbean*. I wanted to pinch myself!

The sun was shining, and I had a butterfly feeling in my chest as I took out the breakfast that Cole's chef had prepared. It was some oatmeal concoction with a ton of fresh fruit, and it was *delish*. I sighed happily as I ate it, looking out at the glittering harbor below.

But the butterfly feeling in my chest soon gave way to a sensation I was all too familiar with. It got sharper, edged with anxiety. Time on my own, without the benefit of Cole's hand on my ass and nine rum punches, meant time to reflect.

I really hated this part of the job.

Cole was the best and the worst client I'd ever had. He was the best because he was the most handsome, the richest, the most fun, the easiest to get along with, the kindest, and the best in bed, courtesy of his rock-hard body and magic cock. He was so amazing, he was ridiculous.

He was so amazing, he was awful. Because never had I ever had feelings for a client before. If I was being honest with myself, which I was not, never had I ever had feelings like this for any man before. But Cole was different, and that's why he was both my greatest dream and my worst nightmare.

He was mine, but only for a little while longer.

I wasn't one to sit around feeling sorry for myself. I'd never had space in my life to be that indulgent. When I was little, I'd learned the hard way. If I dared cry over something that had happened, it only meant more trouble for me.

And I had enough trouble.

But for a moment, I let myself wish things could be different. I let my thoughts become wishes, and I let them carry me away. I wished that instead of his neighbors trying to get Cole evicted because I was a prostitute, they'd invited us to a dinner party. Instead of Todd and Evie getting married today, it was Cole and me. I would wear a gorgeous white dress, and no matter what bad things I'd done in my life, it would all be washed away. I'd be safe. I'd be Cole's wife. And he would love and protect me, in sickness and health, till death did us part.

And then, even though it twisted my heart, I pictured the things I usually thought about when I was trying to escape. The dogs I might get, the Pitbull or the Rottie and the fat BFF mutt sidekick—picket fences, well-tended yards, kids playing on a swing set, sunshine, and lemonade.

But this time, I thought about having those things with Cole.

That thin weed of hope, the one I could never eradicate, stretched out toward the light. I could feel it in my heart. It was the part of me that never gave up—not on myself or my dreams, no matter how farfetched they might be.

Don't do it, girl, said the voice in my head. *Don't do it to yourself.*

Sighing, I cleaned up my dishes and headed for the shower. The voice was right, and I knew it.

That didn't make it hurt any less.

COLE DIDN'T SAY anything about his meeting when he got back. Instead, he climbed into the shower with me and started washing my hair. "I missed you," Cole said. He sounded surprised and maybe a little off-kilter.

"I missed you too, handsome." I smiled as he massaged my hair, the lather running down between us. "It's a beautiful day, huh? A nice day for the wedding. I'm happy for them." I kept my tone light. My billionaire client wasn't paying me to have an emotional breakdown; he was paying me to be a fun, sexy date.

I stepped closer to him. "How about I wash you?"

Cole's eyes were hooded as I grabbed his wicked-expensive shower gel and rubbed it across his enormous, chiseled chest. His glorious cock, which had been at half-mast arousal, sprang fully to life. Pure female satisfaction welled inside me as my hands roamed lower, soaping his amazing rock-hard abs and bulging thigh muscles.

"Mmm, that feels good." Cole closed his eyes, finally seeming to relax into my touch.

I lifted myself on my tiptoes and brushed my lips against his just as my hands circled his thick, erect cock. He moaned again, his tongue seeking mine as I started to milk him. The thing about sex with Cole? It was real natural. Like, I never had to ask him what he wanted, and he never had to tell me what to do. And vice versa. We just moved together, our bodies instinctively anticipating each other's desires in time.

He flexed his hips and deepened the kiss. I increased

the pressure of my hands, rubbing his hard length from base to tip. He thrust again, grunting. I reached down and stroked his balls just the way he liked, grinning to myself. I loved that I knew just how to touch him, how to please him. It made me feel like a billion dollars.

I got down on my knees and milked him, massaging his balls in time with his thrusts. He gave himself over to me, head thrown back, the cords in his neck standing out as I pleasured him. "Fuck, babe," he moaned. *"Yes."* He started thrusting harder, and I increased the pressure, squeezing him enough so that he went wild. It didn't take long. He orgasmed hard, cursing and shuddering, his hands deep in my wet hair.

When he came to, he pulled me up to my feet. We collapsed against the shower wall together, his arms wrapped around me. He kissed me tenderly, again and again—on my lips, my cheeks, my shoulders, the top of my head. For some weird reason, I wanted to cry. What was my problem? It was just a handy in the shower!

"Thank you, Jenny." He pulled me closer. "Thank you."

It sounded like maybe he was thanking me for more than just playing with his balls, but I couldn't be sure.

"Anytime, Coley." My tone was light, but as I clung to his chest, the hot water pouring over us, I felt heavy. I wanted to stay like that forever, safe in our luxury shower cocoon.

That didn't stop me from plastering a smile onto my face as I pulled him in for another playful kiss. I grinned as I grabbed the shower gel and ran my hands up and down his fantastic body. His magic penis started to stiffen again—like I said, it was magic!

I grinned at him as I wrapped my hands around his hardening length. "Come again, as they say," I joked.

"What are you doing to me, babe?" he asked, but he knew. Of course, he knew; this was me and him, him and me. It felt like we were made for each other. Cole threw his head back as he relaxed again, giving himself over to my touch.

"You're fucking incredible," he said.

"I know," I said, and I meant it. I might not be forever, but he would never forget me.

I was going to make damn sure of that.

CHAPTER 22
Cole

I don't know how I found the strength to button my dress shirt and drag on my suit. Jenny had been relentless that morning, not that I was complaining. We'd fooled around in the shower, on the bathroom vanity, and finally, the bed—after we'd collapsed onto it. Jenny's smoking-hot body and our respective multiple orgasms were a welcome distraction from my conversation with my father that morning.

Of all the awful things he'd said to me, only one hurt. *Your mother would be so upset if she could see you now.*

Was that true? Would my mother be ashamed of me?

I was a billionaire. I'd reached the zenith of professional success. My father was correct that I'd never brought a girlfriend home for the holidays, or ever, for that matter.

But that's because (a) after my mother died, my house was depressing AF, and (b) I liked living a life free from attachments. Was there something wrong with that?

I heard Jenny in the bathroom. The blow-dryer was firing on all cylinders as she belted out "Hips Don't Lie" by Shakira. I laughed as I tied my tie. My father's words cut me, but Jenny's determined cheerfulness buoyed me again.

I vowed to forget about the meeting with my father and enjoy the day. Jenny and I were going on that vacation, dammit. I'd deal with my dad after that.

And if he wanted to leave his vast fortune to the bitter Windsor sisters and my disgruntled ex-coach? That was his problem. It was the stupidest thing I'd ever heard, so I doubted he'd follow through on the threat. It was most likely an empty one. Still, I made a mental note to buy out the Windsor's condo as soon as possible. I planned to enjoy having more money than them while I could.

My phone buzzed with a text from Kevin.

> Your father says he expects some kind of a response from you.

> He didn't share the details of your meeting with me, so I'm not sure what he's looking for…

> …but I will say he's as mad as I've ever seen him.

> I know you have to keep texting me as part of your job.
>
> But I'm not responding for the next week.
>
> I'm going on vacation—I'll deal with him later.

Consider yourself sent to spam

I hoped that I wouldn't get Kevin fired. My father was notorious for shooting the messenger. Still, Kevin had worked for the old man for years and remained relatively unscathed or, at least, employed.

I decided it wasn't my problem. My father was mad that I'd hired an escort. He was worried that my arrangement would somehow impact our family's reputation.

Those things were his problem, not mine.

My father was a lot of things, but reckless wasn't one of them. He was bluffing about my inheritance. He had to be.

I refused to think about it any further.

I focused on Jenny singing in the bathroom, then got back to the business of tying my tie.

Jenny stepped out of the bedroom with the gown on. It was strapless, a greenish-blue, fitted precisely to her curves. As promised, she'd swept her into an elegant updo. The hairstyle showed off her jawline and impossibly gorgeous face. She was so pretty, it almost hurt to look at her.

I put my hand over my heart. "Babe. You look incredible." Why the hell did I feel tears welling in my eyes?

She beamed at me. "You look real nice too, Cole. Real nice."

We both stood there awkwardly for a moment. Some sort of heavy feeling swelled in the room, a palpable energy, but I didn't know what it was.

"I have a little something for you," I told her.

"You already bought me this dress and the shoes," Jenny started to argue.

"That's right, and there's more. Because I want to spoil you." I grabbed her hand and led her back to the bedroom.

She eyed the bed, and I chuckled. "The surprise is not my dick, Jenny. My dick's tired. Very tired."

She laughed, the honking sound I'd come to love. "Okay, Coley. I wasn't sure. You're a machine, ya know?"

"Oh, I know." But I was painfully aware that I was human, not a machine—as evidenced by my nerves thrumming. I pulled the small, wrapped box from my dresser. "This is for you."

"What is it?" She carefully took the gift from me.

"A surprise." I watched as she gently removed the wrapping paper as if she feared ripping it. When she opened the velvet box, her jaw dropped open.

"These are... These are gorgeous, Cole. Holy shit! Are they *real*?"

It was my turn to laugh. "Yes, they're emeralds. I thought they'd look so pretty on you with that dress."

"These are *emeralds*? You bought me ginormous emerald earrings?" She gaped at me.

"Try them on." I smiled at her.

"Woah, I don't know about this." She started breathing hard and fanning herself. "These are too expensive."

"No, they're not. Just try them on," I insisted.

Jenny winced. "Cole, I wear fake gold studs from Walmart. The kind that turn your earlobes green."

She tried to hand the box back. "I got no business wearin' earrings like this. I'd be scared to death to lose them."

"They're insured, babe. You don't have to worry about that."

Her face screwed up, confused. "Earrings can have insurance? I don't even have insurance!"

I blew out a deep breath. "Remind me to do something about that. In the meantime, we're late. Can you please try the earrings on? For me?"

"All right, Coley. Since you bought them insurance, and everything." She hustled to the mirror and carefully secured the teardrop emerald earrings. Then she looked at herself, straightening her shoulders and holding her chin up.

It occurred to me that Jenny was a very brave person.

"These are beautiful," she said. "And you're right—they look great with the dress."

"They look great on *you*. You're so beautiful, Jenny. You're the prettiest girl in the whole world."

"Now you sound like Shirley." She winked at me in the mirror, then returned her gaze to her reflection. "I'm ready. I've never been to a society wedding before, you know that? I was nervous, but now I feel good. Actually, I feel like a princess. Thank you, Cole."

"Thank *you*." My heart swelled with pride as I offered her my arm, and she took it.

Then my fake date and I headed out to the society event of the season.

Trinity Church was located in Copley Square. The stately stone church edifice rose into the sky. It was surrounded by skyscrapers and office buildings, which made it seem quaint. The driver dropped us off in front, and I held Jenny's hand as we walked inside. Everyone stopped and stared at my date. She was majestic in her mermaid gown, the large teardrop emeralds sparkling at her ears.

I briefly wondered what my father would think when he saw these photos of me with Jenny. Then I decided that I didn't give a shit.

We headed inside the main chamber of the already crowded church. The beauty of the interior was stunning. Sunlight streamed through the stained-glass windows, and the ceiling soared above us.

"This looks like something out of a fairy tale," Jenny whispered.

"I know. It's perfect." I found an open pew close to the front and helped her slide down the smooth wooden bench. Jenny elicited more stares from the already-seated guests. Hot pride bloomed in my chest as I held her hand, clearly marking the prettiest girl in the world as mine.

James and Audrey came in a few minutes later. James sported a tuxedo, and Audrey wore a pale yellow dress. Her hair was also up in an elegant bun. In a million years, you would never guess that my date and James's were escorts who were barely scraping by in the real world. They looked like royalty.

James hustled Audrey down the aisle, looking flushed. He deposited her with us and then charged off to find Todd. He was the best man, and he was late. I made a mental note not to have him be my best man. Not that I was ever going to need a best man. Or that I'd ever planned on needing one. Sighing, I pushed the thoughts away and watched as Jenny and Audrey hugged it out.

"Hey, Dre!" Jenny pulled Audrey in for a hug.

Audrey stared at her friend when they broke apart, taking in the gown and earrings. "You are stunning."

"Aw, thanks Dre. I guess I clean up okay," Jenny said, beaming at her in pleasure. "Cole bought the dress for me. And the earrings."

Audrey looked past Jenny to me. "That was nice."

I grinned at her. "It was my pleasure. Jenny looks beautiful." I clasped Jenny's hand again, then gave her a quick kiss. Audrey's approval made me feel happy. Jenny smiled. I smiled.

Audrey watched us, a knowing look on her face.

Todd and his attendants came out. Todd was beaming, obviously happy and excited. James looked less so, but at least he'd calmed down a little. He shot Audrey a look, and her cheeks flushed. I wondered just what was up with them. I leaned across Jenny. "I still can't believe he ate that crab cake, Audrey," I said.

"Huh?" She blinked at me, surprised.

"The crab cake you fed James. That first night I met you," I said. "He hates crab. Loathes it."

"I didn't know," she said, sheepish. "He didn't say anything."

I looked at her for a beat. "He must be completely in love with you." Maybe it wasn't my business, but I knew it was true. And I was feeling reckless. Actually, I was feeling lots of things, but reckless was toward the top of the list.

Jenny watched in interest as Audrey sat there, gaping. A deep blush crept up Audrey's neck. "S'okay, Dre," Jenny said, patting her arm. "It's gonna be okay. Close your mouth—you look so pretty, you don't wanna get drool on that dress."

She followed Jenny's orders and closed her mouth, but Audrey still looked stunned. Oh boy. "I didn't mean to make you upset," I said.

"You didn't make me upset," Audrey said. She sounded like a robot.

"Dre doesn't think it's possible that James has feelings for her—she doesn't believe in fairy tales. She's a realist," Jenny explained.

"Of course it's possible," I said recklessly, but now I only had eyes for Jenny.

"Oh, Coley," she said, throwing her arms around my neck. She kissed me, and I forgot all about crab cakes, blabbing about my best friend's feelings, and shutting my mouth. I lost myself in Jenny, savoring the sweet taste of her mouth until the man behind me cleared his throat.

We finally broke apart. "I forgot we were in church," I whispered.

"Me too, Coley." Jenny fanned herself. "Me too."

We focused on the wedding to avoid ripping each other's clothes off in the pew. The enormous church was now packed, filled with beautifully dressed society people. I recognized the mayor as well as several prominent CEOs. The music started, and the Prestons led the wedding processional. Mr. Preston looked refined in his suit. The recently Botoxed Mrs. Preston looked like something out of madam Tussauds wax museum in a glittering, silver-beaded gown secured at the waist with an enormous diamond brooch.

Nine bridesmaids were next—first, Evie's cousins, Meghan, Michelle, and Sarah, their biceps popping as they clutched their bouquets. Then there were some of Evie's friends I recognized from the parties we'd attended, the young women who'd been drinking with Jenny. The bridesmaids' dresses were simple, black, strapless, and obviously couture. Next, Evie came down the aisle with her father. I'd never given her looks much thought, but she was a beautiful bride.

Todd watched his bride-to-be as she headed toward them. There were tears in his eyes, but he was smiling. Evie reached him, and they clasped their hands together, joy apparent on both faces. I clutched Jenny's hand tighter, pulling her against my side.

Easy, bro. Getting emotional did not suit me. Getting emotional and reckless was a recipe for disaster.

"Jenny," Audrey suddenly turned around and whispered. "I have to go. It's an emergency. Tell James I'll meet him at the reception."

"*What?*" Jenny asked. The couple was about to recite their vows. People turned to stare at us.

"It's my *mother*," Audrey hiss-whispered.

"Oh fuck, Dre. Go," Jenny said. "I'll cover for you."

Audrey hitched her dress up and ran from the church.

"What the hell was that about?" I whispered.

"Tell you later, Coley." Jenny shifted uncomfortably in the pew. "But let's just say it's a shit show, all right?"

"All right." I held her hand as the officiant began speaking.

Next to the groom, James's expression became stormy

—he'd seen Audrey run out. James turned and handed something to the groomsman behind him, his cousin. I only realized afterward that he'd given him the rings.

Then he hustled off behind a large velvet curtain, leaving us all wondering just what the hell was going on.

CHAPTER 23
Jenny

THE WEDDING STARTED OFF GREAT. EVIE WAS SO beautiful, I couldn't even believe it. She looked like a fairy-tale princess. So many guests had on amazing dresses; I stared at all of them. They were the best-dressed people I'd ever seen! But Audrey stole the show. Her pale yellow gown was fitted and long, and the beading around the waist showcased her knock-out figure. She was perfect. She looked like she belonged at a society wedding, that she belonged in James's world.

I was feeling happy, real happy. Cole was holding my hand, and that felt good. Audrey was sitting next to me, and that was nice. I was nervous about my dress, of course. I worried I might rip it. And I was nervous about the earrings, that I might lose one. But as they had insurance, I tried not to fret too much. Plus, everyone kept looking at me the way I was looking at them: like they liked my dress. Like they thought I looked pretty.

It felt good. Real good.

Cole said something to Audrey about James eating a crab cake. Like, that James hated crab, but he ate it 'cause Audrey liked it. Cole hadn't told me about that, but it validated what I thought, that James was in love with Audrey. Cole said that, too. That James must be in love with her since he ate a crab cake.

Audrey looked flabbergasted. I patted her back, then explained to Cole,

"Dre doesn't think it's possible that he has feelings for her—she doesn't believe in fairy tales. She's a realist."

"Of course it's possible," he said.

And then he looked at me funny. Real funny.

The butterflies in my chest went bananas, circling, swooping, and having what felt like a little party right there inside me. Was he saying *he* believed in fairy tales? Like, that a hooker and a billionaire could fall in love and live happily ever after?

"Oh, Coley!" I grabbed him and pulled him in for a deep kiss. The butterflies weren't the only things going bananas. I couldn't get enough of him. Cole ran his hands down my shoulders, setting my bare skin on fire. We both pulled away, breathing hard. I vowed to look straight ahead at the ceremony and only straight ahead at the ceremony, so help me God. We didn't need to be groping each other on a church pew!

But then Audrey gasped. She turned white.

"Jenny," she turned to me and whispered. "I have to go. It's an emergency. Tell James I'll meet him at the reception."

"What?" I asked too loud. The people in the pew in front of us turned around to stare.

"It's my *mother*," Audrey hiss-whispered.

"Oh fuck, Dre. Go. I'll cover for you."

She was running down the aisle in a flash, chasing her wicked old witch of a mother out of the church. And then James, who was the best man, followed her. I mean, I couldn't see that he followed her, but he hustled behind the curtain and didn't return for the rest of the ceremony.

Good thing Todd and Evie were so busy making goo-goo eyes at each other that they didn't seem to notice. But I saw Celia Preston turn around, and I knew that bitch didn't miss a trick. *Uh-oh*. Celia Preston wouldn't be happy that her son, the best man, had run out before the wedding vows to chase Audrey. She *really* wouldn't be happy if she knew the truth, that not only had James run out after her, that Audrey was an escort from the wrong side of the tracks, and that her billionaire son was more than likely falling in love with her.

Oops.

I'd promised Audrey I'd cover for her, and I would. But for the moment, there was nothing I could do. Cole and I sat and watched the ceremony, our hands entwined. I loved weddings, and they usually made me cry, even the ones on TV, but I was too worried about my friend to get emotional. Audrey's mother was bad news. She made James's mother look civilized, which was saying something. She'd come into AccommoDating's office once, demanding money, and Elena had to throw her ass out.

The happy couple recited their vows. I watched as Evie slid the ring onto Todd's finger, and he did the same for her. The officiant pronounced them man and wife, and then Todd pulled Evie in for a big, fat kiss.

Everyone cheered.

As soon as the ceremony ended, I moved fast. I checked my phone, but there was nothing. I tried calling Dre—no answer. I hustled outside, but everyone was gone. Cole rushed out after me. "James didn't answer his phone," he said.

"Dre didn't, either." I scowled as Mr. and Mrs. Preston came outside. Celia was scanning the crowd, looking for her older son.

I pulled Cole next to them. "Audrey and James are meeting us at the reception," I said, loud enough for Celia to hear. "Audrey just got her period. She had to get out of here so she didn't wreck her dress."

Cole coughed. Celia Preston's eyeballs looked like they might pop out of her head.

"Sucks, I know," I continued for good measure. "'Specially because we're all going to the Caribbean tomorrow!"

Celia's brow furrowed—or at least, it looked like she tried to furrow it. Tough to tell with all the filler. "Excuse me. Did you say you are coming on the trip with us?" she asked.

"Yes, ma'am." I smiled inwardly when she cringed at being called *ma'am*. "Coley and I are lookin' forward to it."

"We are really lookin' forward to it, Mrs. Preston." Cole waggled his eyebrows at her. "Beautiful ceremony, by the way."

"Yes." She cleared her throat, sounding as though she was about to gag. "Quite."

COLE and I snuck away and headed for the reception. We made three calls apiece to James and Audrey, and still no answer. "I hope they're okay, and Audrey's mom left them alone."

"I'm sure it's fine. James is probably banging Audrey

against a wall somewhere," Cole surmised. As usual, he sounded confident.

"Could be," I agreed. But I had a pit in my stomach.

"What's wrong with her mother?" Cole asked. "She can't possibly be worse than Celia Preston."

I snorted. "She'd give Old Celia a run for her money."

"Really?" Cole looked confused. "How is that even possible?"

"Eh, she's down on her luck—always had been. Audrey said she's a grifter. She's been in trouble with the police, too. Drunk driving, walking out on bar tabs—you name it, Mama's done it."

Cole stared straight ahead. "Audrey's so...normal. She seems like a genuinely nice person. How does that happen?"

I raised my eyebrows, calculating an answer. Suppose Cole had any idea what *my* family was like...yikes. He'd be surprised at how "normal" I was, too. Finally, I laughed, but it sounded as fake as it felt. "Real easy. It happens real easy."

He stared at me, but I didn't elaborate. "It was nice what you said to Audrey, you know. About the crab cake."

He nodded. "It's true. The first night I met her, she fed James a crab cake. He literally hates them—it's a thing. So when he told me he'd eaten one because she'd fed it to him, I almost fell over dead. I knew then. He had it bad for her."

Cole went quiet for a minute. "Audrey doesn't think that they're going to keep dating after this?"

I got a prickly feeling in the back of my neck. "She doesn't think it can work out," I admitted.

"What do you think?" He seemed like he was holding his breath.

"I think Audrey's special. I think James would be crazy to let her go. But that's me, and I'm not exactly a realist." I shrugged.

"I agree with you," Cole said. "I think Audrey's special, and James would be crazy to let her go, too."

The car got very quiet. I didn't know what to say for a minute, so I didn't say anything. Neither did Cole. The silence stretched out between us, and I felt awkward for the first time since I'd met him.

"What're we gonna do if they aren't at the reception?" I asked, eventually. "I'm going to have to come up with something better than Audrey being on her period!"

Cole laughed. "True, but that was quick thinking on your part. How about we say she has a headache because she's on her period?"

Hearing Cole say "on her period" made me honk-laugh. "That's good, Coley. That's real good."

I held his hand and my breath for the rest of the ride to the reception. I knew where we were going—to the formal party, then on a plane to the Caribbean tomorrow—but I didn't know where we were *going* going.

If anywhere. I don't know why I was even wondering about it; when our time was up, I'd go back to Accommo-Dating. Cole would return to his real life, filled with Victoria's Secret models, hockey, and venture-capitaling.

I wasn't exactly a realist. But I wasn't dumb, either. Fairy tales might come true for Audrey because she was a good girl. But for a girl like me?

I knew better than to believe in happy endings.

CHAPTER 24
Cole

INTROSPECTION WAS NOT IN MY NATURE, YET I found myself quiet on the ride to the reception. Several things were hitting me at once. First of all, James was clearly in love with Audrey. He'd never been a fan of his family, but running out on Todd's wedding was still wildly out of character. He'd left because he was in love with his escort.

And he wasn't the only one.

I wondered what my mom would have thought about Jenny. Probably, she would've loved her. Like Jenny, my mother was a warm person—the opposite of my father. If a stranger sneezed near us, she was the first one to always say, "God bless you." That was one of the small, funny things I remembered about her. She was always smiling.

She smiled at everyone in the grocery store and when we walked down the street. People always smiled back.

When I lost her, I lost my smile—my real one. But I felt like since I'd met Jenny, it had somehow come back.

I'd never been serious about a woman before. I had zero interest in forming attachments; I'd always believed a romantic relationship would weigh me down. But I didn't feel that way about Jenny. Because she was an escort, she was wildly different from the wealthy society women I usually "dated," if that's what you could even call it. But it was more than that. Jenny wasn't the type of person that you got to know—she just sort of happened to you.

Me. She'd just sort of happened to me. And I didn't know what that meant, except that I couldn't quite remember what I was doing before I met her.

And I had zero idea what I'd do after her job ended, and she was long gone.

Luckily, James was at the reception. But Audrey was nowhere in sight. Jenny went to the ladies' room while I found my friend at the bar, double-fisting bourbons. Without a word, he handed me one. I watched, alarmed, as he knocked his back and immediately ordered another.

"What happened?" I asked. "Where's Audrey?"

"She quit." He ordered another drink.

I didn't understand. "She quit...?"

"*Me*. She quit me."

"Oh fuck, James. Are you serious?"

He shrugged. "I'm serious about getting shit-faced."

"What're you going to tell everyone?" I asked. "We're supposed to go on the trip tomorrow."

"I told Todd she's sick." He eyed his crystal tumbler, assessing the amber liquid inside. "I've decided that, for tonight, this is how I'm handling it."

"I'm sorry. That sucks."

"You're telling me." He held up his glass. "Anyway, *cheers*. To Todd and Evie. I hope somebody around here lives happily fucking ever after."

"Uh...yeah." I tipped my glass toward his. "That's quite the toast."

He muttered something unintelligible. Before James could order another bourbon, I pulled him away from the bar into a quiet corner. "What happened? Why'd she leave? I thought things were going great."

He shrugged. "Her mother showed up at the wedding. Did Jenny tell you?"

I nodded. "She said the mother's bad news."

"That's an understatement."

"What did she want? Why did she try and crash the wedding?"

"She's after money. I've given her plenty to shut her up, but she keeps threatening me to get more. But I handled her today." James sounded sure of himself. "She won't be back."

"But still, Audrey's upset?" I asked.

"Yes, she's beating herself up about it," James said. "She said she had no business accepting the job in the first place and that she's put me in danger."

"She quit because she wants to protect you," I deduced.

"Exactly. She thinks she's not good enough for me. She says her mother will keep coming back and that it's not safe for me to be with her," he sighed. "Don't tell me Jenny's pulling the same crap with you."

"We haven't gotten that far," I admitted. "Jenny hasn't told me anything about her past."

"Interesting," James said. "Maybe she's better off than the rest of us and doesn't have one."

"That'd be a neat trick," I agreed. "But I don't think she's that lucky."

"Probably not." James downed the rest of his bourbon.

The prospect of watching my friend drink until he fell over wasn't very appealing. Suddenly, I felt tired. I wanted to find Jenny and just go home. "We're probably going to head out early—hope that's okay."

"I'd do the same thing if I had someone to go home with," James said gloomily. "You'll be there tomorrow, though, right?"

"Of course. I'm not going to abandon you with your family on vacation. Plus, Jenny's excited. She's never been to the Caribbean before."

"Neither has Audrey." He sounded like he might cry.

I regarded my friend. "You might want to lay off the bourbon," I counseled.

"Fuck you, Bryson," he said as he ambled back toward the bar.

At least he was acting a little like himself. It made me feel slightly less guilty as I abandoned him and searched the party for Jenny. She'd returned from the ladies' and was drinking with the bridesmaids, who were all interchangeably thin and blond, except for one lone brunette. Jenny said something that made them all laugh.

"Your girlfriend is adorable," cooed one of them, a non-descriptively pretty blond. "And she sure can party! Where did you two meet?"

I coughed. I knew the Madam had supplied us with a background story, but I couldn't remember it.

Jenny nudged me. "The gym! Don't you remember,

babe? I was on the treadmill next to yours, and you couldn't stop starin' at my ass."

"I was mesmerized by it." I grinned. "Still am."

"Nice," said the bridesmaid, her voice wistful.

"You guys goin' on the trip tomorrow?" Jenny asked the bridesmaids.

"Hell yes!" said the brunette. "I cannot wait!"

"Me either," Jenny said eagerly. "I've never been to the Caribbean before."

All of Evie's bridesmaids were rich, just like her. They looked at Jenny like she had three heads. "You've never been to the Caribbean?" The blonde closest to us sounded baffled.

"Never."

"Girl, we are going to have a good time! We're going to drink rum out of coconuts and get wild!" The brunette raised her drink, and they all hollered, "Cheers!"

"Let's do shots!" one of Evie's cousins shouted.

They stampeded toward the bar. Celia Preston, who had just entered the room, gaped at the herd of hooting, hollering, already tipsy young women. She grabbed a martini from a passing server, then watched as they ordered rounds of shots and downed them.

"Jenny, are you ready to get out of here?" I asked.

"Sure." She looked longingly at the crowded bar for a

moment, then smiled. "I have all week to teach these whipper-snappers a thing or two."

"That's my girl." I grabbed her hand. While Celia Preston was sipping her martini and scowling at the partying bridesmaids, and James was leaning against the bar with a fresh drink and a thunderous expression, we took the opportunity to sneak away.

"They're all going to be seriously hung over in the morning, including James," I said once we were safely in the car. "Did you talk to Audrey?"

"Nah, she wouldn't pick up. What happened, anyway?"

"James said she quit."

"*What?*" Jenny looked panicked. "She can't do that! She needs the money for Tommy, he's in a group home, and they can't afford to keep him in there—"

"Woah, easy. Who's Tommy?"

"Dre's brother," she explained. "He's got special needs, and their mom wasn't looking after him too good. So Audrey found a home for him that's nice, like, top of the line. He likes it there. But it's wicked expensive."

I made a mental note to give Audrey money for these expenses, then realized James wouldn't hear of it. He'd probably already taken care of the brother. "I'm sure it will work out. I think maybe they just argued. But I don't know if she'll be coming on the trip tomorrow."

"Oh, this sucks." Jenny frowned and shook her head. "Dre's probably upset that her mother showed up at the wedding. She coulda ruined everything. If the Prestons saw her and put two and two together, it would've been terrible. She's probably mad at herself for the situation, even though it's not her fault. She's probably feeling real bad, you know?"

I reached for her hand. "It's a shame her mother's like that."

"It is." Jenny nodded solemnly. "Dre doesn't deserve that."

We were quiet for a minute. I wanted to ask Jenny about her own family, but I hesitated. After a moment, I asked, "Do you have any brothers or sisters?"

"I have a brother. Don't talk to him, though. He's a drunk."

She said this matter-of-factly as if she was talking about the weather. "Oh. What about your parents?" I asked.

"Um..." She stared out the window. "I never had a lot of parental guidance, I guess you could say. I was pretty much on my own."

"Oh," I said again, lamely.

"Yeah, you know," Jenny said. "People with solid backgrounds don't usually end up hooking, if you know what I mean. It's not exactly aspirational."

Another awkward silence stretched out between us. I

wanted to ask her so many things, but I didn't know how to phrase my questions without sounding like an ass.

"I was a waitress before I was with the agency," Jenny offered. "At the Sizzler in the Theater District. Real classy." She winked at me.

"Did you like it?"

"It fucking sucked," she said immediately. "You ever wait tables? No, of course not. You make, like, two dollars an hour plus tips. I never coulda lived on that."

I put my arm around her. "I'm sorry if things have been hard."

"Nah, you don't need to be sorry, Coley. I'm takin' care of myself. I have a little apartment, and I'm doing just fine, thank you." She sounded a teeny bit defiant.

"Okay, Jenny," I said.

"Okay, Coley," she said and nestled against me. "I'm looking forward to our trip tomorrow. I just hope Audrey makes it, 'cause it'd suck to be the only person there who's never been to the Caribbean before, you know?"

"I know." I kissed the top of her head. I most certainly didn't know since my family had vacationed in St. Bart's every winter since I'd been born. "But you'll have the bridesmaids—they adore you. And you have me."

"Yeah, that's true." She settled against me, and my heart swelled. "And you're pretty good."

"You're pretty good too, Jenny." I pulled her closer against me, inhaling her coconut-y scent.

I wondered what I would've done in James's position had Jenny run off and left me. But then I reminded myself that I wasn't prone to introspection, and I thanked God for that.

CHAPTER 25
Jenny

I PULLED MY FEDORA DOWN ARTFULLY TO THE side as I checked myself in the mirror. The black jumpsuit Shirley had bought me was luxurious, and the hat was the perfect accessory. I looked like one of those rich women I saw periodically driving a Range Rover around town. Hot, wealthy, and in charge. I would fit in just fine with the five-star resort crowd. I hoped. With a nod of approval at my reflection and a reminder to fake it until I make-d it, I grabbed my carry-on bag.

Audrey still hadn't texted me by the time Cole and I headed to Logan Airport. It made me feel funny worrying about my friend; usually, it was the other way around. And that wasn't the only thing making me feel weird.

All of a sudden, things were slightly off between Cole

and me. No one would notice it but me. Maybe not even Cole. On the surface, everything appeared fine. Actually, it seemed to be great. We'd still had sex when we got home from the reception. I still did the thing with his balls. We both orgasmed, yelling and grunting in pleasure and held each other while we fell asleep. Still, something was amiss.

Something wasn't right.

I'd felt oddly comfortable with Cole from the beginning. It shouldn't have been that way. We were from two different worlds, but somehow, the billionaire bachelor had immediately put me at ease. The attraction had been instantaneous. The sex made me feel like a million bucks—scratch that, a billion. Same thing whenever Cole put his arm around me and when I woke up next to his big, warm body. I was proud to be next to him. Real proud, like I was being rewarded for good behavior, and everyone could see it.

But now, as we headed to Logan for our flight, another awkward silence stretched out between us. I wondered if it was because the vacation was the last part of the assignment. All of a sudden, the end of our arrangement was in sight. The party was about to be over. Instead of crying about it, I vowed to enjoy myself. Maybe the trip wouldn't be the end of us after all. Maybe Cole would decide to "buy" me and put me up in a condo or something. Maybe he'd become a regular.

Or maybe pigs would fly.

Again, I promised myself I wouldn't think about it. I had plenty to be happy about. We were flying to the Caribbean! Shirley had gone shopping for me, dropping off a week's worth of designer resort wear in addition to the things Elena had already packed. I had the hottest billionaire alive sitting beside me, holding my hand. We were going to go swimming in turquoise water and drink rum out of coconuts. I should enjoy my dreams coming true, not cry about whatever happened next. Or whatever didn't happen next.

"We're flying private," Cole announced after we went through security.

"Woah. Seriously—a whole plane for just us?"

"Yep." Cole smiled, pleased at my reaction. It was like the sun coming out. "You're going to love it."

"Of course I'm going to freaking love it!" I grinned back at him. "I'm flying private to the Caribbean with my billionaire boyfriend. What's not to love?'

He grabbed me and pulled me against him, some of the uneasiness between us dissipating. "We're going to have so much fun, babe. I can't wait to see you in some of those bikinis Shirley bought."

I arched my eyebrows. "You're going to be seeing a lot of me." Shirley had bought scraps of fabric—thin, lacy scraps—sold as expensive swimwear. Celia Preston was going to get an eyeful!

Speaking of the Preston matriarch, we soon found her in the waiting area, along with Robert Preston, Todd and Evie, Evie's cousins and their husbands, the other bridesmaids, and a small crowd of additional well-dressed guests who I'd seen at the various events. Our private seating area was hushed. The guests were silently drinking their coffee, bleary-eyed and most likely quite hungover from the reception.

James and Audrey weren't there yet. I crossed my fingers, hoping they'd make it.

"Mrs. Preston. Mr. Preston." Cole nodded at them as we took seats near Todd and Evie. The happy couple smiled at us. Todd raised his coffee in a cheer.

"It was an awesome wedding," I said. From her perch several seats away, Celia Preston sighed. "*Wicked* awesome," I added for good measure.

Evie grinned. "Thanks! I agree." She snuggled against Todd, putting her hand on his chest. Her enormous diamond winked at me.

I briefly wondered what it would feel like to be married and have a ginormous ring on my finger, but I shoved the thought away. *Eye on the ball, Jenny,* I reminded myself. *Eye on Cole's balls!* I was getting paid a fuck-ton of money for this assignment. There was no reason to sit around, waiting to board a private plane, boo-hooing and feeling sorry for myself.

A minute later, James and Audrey arrived. My friend looked pale beneath her makeup. James appeared tense, his hands clenched into fists at his sides. *Uh-oh.* Gone were the goo-goo eyes and the lovey-dovey behavior from the past week. They both looked uncomfortable as they approached our group.

Celia rose as soon as she saw them. "Audrey, dear, we were worried you weren't going to make it. What happened to you last night?" she asked. "I would have asked my son at the reception, but he avoided me like the plague, as usual."

Audrey offered a strained smile. "I wasn't feeling well, Mrs. Preston. I'm so sorry I had to leave—I missed everything. James said it was extraordinary."

"You're better this morning?" Celia Preston eyed her up and down.

Fine actress that she was, Audrey reached for James's hand. "I'm much better, thank you. I'm really looking forward to this trip." She almost sounded convincing.

Seemingly satisfied, Celia went to sit back down. But then she stopped herself. "Oh, I meant to ask you—who was that strange woman you were talking to yesterday at the church? She caused quite a stir in the back, I understand."

Audrey's smile faltered, but only for a moment. "She was just some woman who wandered in off the street—I didn't want her interrupting the ceremony. So I helped her out."

Celia Preston managed to raise one eyebrow slightly, and her gaze shifted to her son. "And you left your brother's wedding to go help Audrey with this random stranger?"

James shrugged. "I wanted to make sure Audrey didn't need me. Turns out she didn't. She handled it all on her own."

"How impressive. You almost make it sound as if Audrey's an actual adult." Celia chuckled meanly and sat back down.

Cole and I watched this exchange with interest. "She really is a bitch, huh?" I whispered. "She and Audrey's mom deserve each other."

"Maybe we should invite Audrey's mom to the island, too," he said, also keeping his voice low. "Then we can vote them both off."

"I like the way you think, Coley," I said, feeling myself relax a little. I might have awkwardness to deal with, but it was nothing compared to what Audrey was going through. I needed to buck up and support my friend.

Cole smiled at me. "We make a pretty good team, don't you think?"

I grinned back. "I sure do." I could feel the hope rising in my chest, that pesky weed that cropped up regardless of its surroundings. Mentally, I plucked it. It was time to keep my eye on the ball. *The balls.*

I had work to do, not the least of which was helping my best friend.

THE PRIVATE PLANE was impressively luxurious, of course. The chairs were wide and comfortable-looking, with plenty of space to spread out. We followed a stiff-looking James and Audrey to the back of the plane, and I sighed in relief that we had a few rows to ourselves. I was psyched to get away from Celia Preston.

We flopped down across the aisle from Audrey and James. I stared at my friend, but she was avoiding me. She probably didn't want to talk, but too bad. That's what friends did.

"Where'd you run off to last night?" I asked. "We had to watch James drown his sorrows in about ten bourbons."

"I had a thing," she said, that same strained smile on her face.

I frowned at Audrey and then turned to James. "Hey, James. Wanna switch seats for a minute?" He nodded, gratefully sliding in next to Cole, who punched him on the arm in greeting.

I turned to Audrey as the flight attendant went through the safety presentation. "What's the matter with you two?" I whispered.

She leaned over to check that James and Cole couldn't hear us; they were deep in conversation. "A lot," she said. She looked miserable. "I'm thinking I just need to be his escort. No more feelings. It's too messy. There's too much at stake."

I raised my eyebrows. "He was a mess last night at the reception, Dre. Seriously. He was miserable without you." Cole had told me how many bourbons James had banged through just at the start of the reception. "And he still looks like that today—like he has an emotional hangover. You need to make that right."

She started fussing with her outfit, a nervous habit. "I don't know if I can do that, Jenny."

"Dre." I waited until she looked up and met my eyes. "Don't you try to fool me. I know you have bona fide feelings for that man."

Audrey raised her chin, looking defiant. "I thought you said thoughts and feelings were invisible, Jenny. No one's supposed to be able to see them."

"They're not invisible when they're written all over your face," I snapped.

We just looked at each other for a beat.

"I'm trying to do the right thing," she said. "For both James and me."

"Did you talk to him about how you're feeling? Did he tell you what he wants?" I asked.

She shook her head. "He tried to. But honestly, I don't want to know. Because no matter what he says, I know I'm not the best thing for him."

I squeezed her arm. "You're such a good person—one of the best people I know. When're you going to give yourself a chance?"

"A chance for what?" she asked miserably.

"To be happy," I said.

"I *am* happy. At least I know what it feels like now," she mumbled.

I frowned at her again. "If you love him—and I'm guessing that's what you mean—you've got to give him a chance," I said.

"I can't, Jenny." Audrey looked like she might start crying. "I'm just trying to keep this from going from bad to worse. Bad is where I'm at. I love him, and he's totally out of my league. His mother hates me, and she'll never accept me into their family. My mother's already tried to blackmail him. That's why she came to the wedding. It's not like we're ever going to be one big, happy family."

She took a deep breath. "And it could get so much worse—that's why I don't even want to know how he feels. What if he loves me back, huh? It'll never work out and that would break my heart. Or what if he doesn't love me back? Then *that* would break my fucking heart. You get it?"

"I get it," I sighed. "But you gotta stop this overthinking. And you gotta let him have a say. Otherwise you'll never find out."

"Find out what?" she asked.

"Who he *is*, Dre." I patted her hand. "If you don't let him tell you how he feels about you, you'll never get a chance to know. And that might seem safe and perfect in that little airtight container that you're trying to create for yourself, but it's not right.

"I know you. You want everything in order. You want to take care of Tommy and keep your mom out of trouble and keep James up on a pedestal. But that little airtight container's not big enough for you, girl. It's not big enough for you to have a *life*."

"Huh," she said. She fussed with her outfit some more. "Have I told you lately that you're smart?"

"You have," I said and smiled. "So if you think I'm so smart, you listen to what I'm saying. You gotta be brave here. Desperate times call for desperate measures. And maybe some liquid courage."

I hit the button above us, and an attendant appeared instantly. "We'd like two large glasses of alcohol," I said. "Any kind you got. This being such a fancy flight and all, I'm sure it's all good."

CHAPTER 26
Cole

JAMES WAS HURTING FROM A NASTY HANGOVER. A faint odor of bourbon wafted from his pores. Still, he seemed more like himself than he had the night before. He had dark circles under his eyes but was definitely more at ease. Maybe because he had managed to get Audrey on the flight, and she couldn't run away from him so easily.

He didn't reveal much as the plane took off and headed toward the Caribbean. However, one piece of crucial information did escape his lips. "I had to drag her back," he admitted, "and I don't even care. It's like I have no fucking pride anymore."

"I think that's what happens when an emotional boner takes on a life of its own," I said.

"Thanks a lot, Cole."

"My pleasure."

James glanced over at Jenny and Audrey, who were deep in conversation. "Enough about me," he said, his voice weary. "What's going on with you two?"

I shrugged. "You know...hot sex, handholding, escorting. The usual."

He arched an eyebrow. "You have no idea what you're doing, do you?"

"Nope," I admitted. I took the opportunity to hit the call button, and a flight attendant materialized, seemingly out of thin air. "Alcohol, please," I ordered. "Lots of it."

James shook his head as she left to get us our drinks. "We can both close multi-million dollar deals without blinking an eye. But when it comes to relationships, we're lost. You might be even worse off than me, and that's saying something."

I leaned back in the comfortable seat. James was insulting me, but he wasn't wrong, and I wasn't upset. But what was I going to do—cry about it?

I vowed then and there to enjoy every second of my vacation. I would ignore my emotional ineptitude, my father, and the chattering voice in my head that wanted to discuss, at length, my intentions and feelings toward my escort.

"Maybe you can level up with your emotional boner, and then you can teach me a thing or two," I suggested. "Until then, we drink."

He scrubbed a hand across his face. "That's going to be a lot of drinking."

"I'll drink to that," I said and grinned.

As we landed on the island and cell service was available again, my phone lit up with messages. With extreme displeasure, I read several texts from Kevin, my father's assistant.

> Mr. Bryson wasn't happy when he saw pictures from the wedding yesterday.
>
> He wants you to call him immediately.
>
> Also, Ramos canceled a meeting with him.
>
> He's going code red, I'm afraid.

Fuck. To say that my father's temper tantrum was happening at a terrible time was an understatement. I was out of the country, most likely with spotty Wi-Fi, and I was on vacation, dammit. I had zero desire to deal with his bad behavior. He'd already threatened me with the loss of my family fortune. What did he want from me—to dump Jenny in a foreign country, swear off escorts for good, and bully Ramos into giving him the approvals?

Taking a deep breath, I texted Kevin back.

> I'll deal with him.
>
> On vacation at the moment. Crappy service.
>
> I'll call him as soon as I'm back in town.

Kevin didn't text me back. I knew what his silence meant. In the short term, he was screwed. My father would undoubtedly unleash his ire on the messenger. But in the long term, I was only screwing myself. If there was one thing my father hated, it was being put on the back burner.

"You workin'?" Jenny asked, nodding toward my phone.

I slid it into my pocket. "I'm telling my associates that everything's on hold till we get back. This week's just for you and me." I grabbed her hand, and she entwined her fingers with mine.

"That's nice, baby," she cooed. She looked so cute in her fedora.

I didn't want to think about my father's temper escalating. It was only going to get worse. I longed to forget about him and just be with Jenny, strip her out of those clothes, and leave nothing but the hat on. A zap of electricity crackled between us. As if she could read my thoughts, Jenny gave me a knowing smile. "I can't wait to see our suite," she said suggestively.

My cock stiffened, and I shifted uncomfortably. I couldn't wait to get to the fucking resort. Thoughts of my father and Kevin went out the window. I only wanted to think about Jenny. "Me either, babe. Me either."

THE ISLAND WAS GORGEOUS; the resort was gorgeous, but all I cared about was hustling Jenny to our *casita* and ripping her clothes off.

"Yes! There's a plunge pool." I fist-pumped into the air, feeling myself already getting hard again.

"Wow," Jenny said. "This place is incredible!" She walked around our little private property, which had walls surrounding the intimate outdoor space. There was a gorgeous small pool—perfect for two—luxurious outdoor furniture and a full bar. The balmy Caribbean breeze swept Jenny's curls over her shoulder. She smiled up at the sun; she smiled at the tropical birds chirping nearby, and she smiled at me. "I'm putting my suit on. I can't wait to get my ass in that pool!"

"Me either," I called. "And leave the hat on!"

Jenny winked at me and disappeared inside, and I counted the seconds until she returned. To her credit, she didn't disappoint. Her rocking body looked spectacular in one of the tiny, black thong bathing suits that Shirley had bought for her. It had cost a small fortune and was abso-fuckinglutely worth it. As instructed, she'd kept the fedora on, and the effect was super-hot. Jenny was sexy, stylish, and utterly confident. To me, she was the prettiest girl in the world.

"You look very vacation-y," I noted as she eased herself into the plunge pool. "And sexy."

"That Shirley really knows how to shop. I gotta send her a thank-you note," Jenny said.

She whooped as she reached the last step and went all the way in, the water suddenly coming up to her shoulders. "Holy crap, they don't call this thing a plunge pool for nothin'!" She laughed her honking laugh, now one of my all-time favorite sounds, then asked, "Can you pour me some champagne? I saw a bottle on ice in the kitchen."

"Your wish is my command."

I hustled inside, eager to fetch her champagne, anxious to get into the pool, desperate to get my hands on her. Jenny was like a drug I had zero intention of quitting. Being with her helped me forget everything else; she was the antidote I hadn't known I needed.

I stripped out of my clothes. I grabbed the champagne bucket and two glasses. Then I strode outside, buck naked.

Jenny pulled her sunglasses down and stared at me.

"That is a big...ice bucket," she joked. My erection was getting larger by the second.

"All the better to serve you with." I winked at her, then poured us each some champagne. I first climbed into the pool with Jenny, shocked at the cold water. I steeled myself against it, praying I didn't suffer shrinkage.

"It's real refreshing," Jenny said. She clinked her glass against mine. "Cheers. To our Caribbean vacation!"

"To our Caribbean vacation." I sipped the fizzy liquid and immediately found Jenny's mouth with mine—I couldn't wait. She groaned with pleasure as our tongues connected. Suddenly, I was no longer worried about shrinkage. The sun shone down on us, the cool water gave me shivers, and the feel of Jenny's skin beneath my touch was incredible.

If there was a heaven, it was a plunge pool in the Caribbean with Jenny.

"Babe." She pulled back and finished her champagne in one swig. "You're very sexy on vacation, you know that?"

"You think so?" I grinned at her. "Let me show you just how sexy I can be." I kissed her again, our tongues connecting, and my whole body radiated with desire. *Holy fuck.* Jenny did something to me; I couldn't even explain it. It could best be described as my base instincts ignited—I needed to take her, to penetrate her deep inside, to make her lose control and scream my name.

I needed to mark her as *mine*.

I wanted to be gentle, to be tender, but our kisses were urgent. I undid her bikini top and was confronted by her perfect breasts, with just the outline of a tan around them. I suckled her nipples greedily, and Jenny moaned beneath me, arching her back. She was kissing me, too—my shoulders and biceps, her fingers trailing down my back.

Jenny knew just what to do. She wrapped her hand around my hard length and started to milk me. *Oh fuck.* My eyes rolled back in my head as I thrust against her tight grip. It felt so good as she applied more pressure, almost pushing me to the edge already. It felt so good, but I didn't want her hands... I couldn't wait. I roughly pulled her bikini to the side, and she guided me against her slit—soaking wet and hot.

I flipped her around and bent her over the side of the pool.

"Yes, Cole," she panted, slightly spreading her legs open. Her glorious ass was on full display for me now. I bent and licked her slit from her clit all the way up. She shivered and moaned beneath me. "Give it to me, babe. Don't make me wait."

I stroked my erection against her, driving us both wild.

She was already so wet I almost came right there. But instead, I was going to give her what she wanted—me. I inched inside her, ensuring she could accommodate every bit of my thickness. She was tight, but she greedily sucked me in, bucking her hips until I notched inside her fully.

Once I was all the way in, I started to drive hard.

Her bathing suit caused friction, rubbing against the base of my shaft. *Fuck!* She reached down and stroked my balls as I pounded into her. The multiple sensations were driving me wild. She was so wet that we slid against each other easily, her muscles clenching and squeezing me, making my whole body shudder.

We'd done it so many times, but never quite like this. The sex was hard, driving, deep. I was giving her everything I had, and she was taking it. "Yes, Cole," she panted. "Fuck. Fuck *me*. That's right, baby. Right there—" She erupted into a scream as she came, hard, her body spasming around me.

Deep, primal satisfaction seared inside me. "Yes baby, scream for me. You're mine. You're fucking *mine*."

I thrust again, harder. My balls were heavy. I wanted to go slow, to make it last. But there was nothing stopping the pressure building inside me. *Oh fuck.* I was going to come so hard, I might go blind. I reached around and fingered her swollen clit as I pounded her. "Oh my God," she moaned. "Cole, Cole—"

She orgasmed again, even more powerfully this time, pushing me over the edge. I buried myself inside her and came hard, shooting my seed deep inside. *"Fuck."* That was the only word for it. I ruthlessly thrust as she continued to spasm around me, crying out for all the Caribbean to hear. Hot pride ran through my veins, and I pumped deliciously inside her, finishing her off, finishing myself off, dying, and being reborn again. This was why they called it coming, I thought, my head zigzagging with pleasure I'd never experienced before: I'd finally arrived.

We collapsed together on the edge of the plunge pool. Jenny's fedora was askew. Her curls were in my face. Her perfect, round ass was pressed against me; the thong bikini still shoved to the side.

I couldn't bring myself to move. That had been the best sex of my life, and it wasn't because of the plunge pool. It wasn't the position—although penetrating her from behind was excellent. It wasn't because of the thong bikini or even the fedora. It was because…Jenny.

It was because it was with Jenny. Something deep inside me welled up, bringing me close to tears. I rested my face against her warm skin, the sun shining down on us, her body rising and falling with each breath.

I love you, I mouthed against her back.

I was either too dumb or too scared to say the words out loud, I didn't know which.

CHAPTER 27
Jenny

I THOUGHT I'D DIED AND GONE TO HEAVEN because Cole had slain me with his magic penis. Ah, to have a man whose cock curved just right! I hadn't known that a G-spot was really a thing until this assignment. Not only was I making great money, I was learning something. Win-win, if you asked me.

And I was definitely winning. The Caribbean resort we were staying at was ten stars—five wouldn't do it justice. Butlers were everywhere in white tuxedos, and the grounds were meticulously groomed. Our private *casita* (that's what Cole called it) was decadently luxurious, and then there was the private plunge pool (need I say more) and the ten bottles of *Veuve* I discovered in the fridge.

Not too shabby.

After mind-blowing, brain-numbing sex, Cole and I showered, took a quick nap, and headed to the pool. My limbs were loose, and I felt utterly, impossibly satisfied. Cole held my hand. He looked so handsome in his swim trunks, showcasing his athletic thighs, and a tight-fitting T-shirt highlighting his bulging forearms and chiseled chest. If he hadn't already fucked me senseless, I'd be dragging him back to the casita for more. But I needed to eat—I had to keep my strength up for that magic penis of his!

The tropical birds chirped in the palm trees, tiny lizards ran across the path, and Cole held my hand as we walked to the pool. It was warm, with a balmy breeze that kept it from being too hot. Once we rounded the corner, I saw the beach. Pristine white sand stretched out on either side, contrasting with crystal-clear turquoise water.

"Oh my God, Coley." I squeezed his hand. "I can't believe the water looks like that! It doesn't seem real."

He grinned. "It's definitely nicer than Boston Harbor. Let's go down and touch the water before we meet up with everyone else, okay?"

"Okay." I put a hand over my heart as we left the path and reached the beach. I stepped out of my flip-flops onto the pillowy white sand. It felt like magic. We walked down to the water, and I fell in love as soon as my feet touched it. It was warm but refreshing. It didn't hurt, unlike the freezing ocean water back home. "This is incredible."

Cole squeezed my hand. "I like seeing it through your eyes," he said. "It's special."

I glanced at him. He was the most handsome, most charming, most everything, most Cole I'd ever met. I would never say it aloud, but the water wasn't the only thing I'd fallen in love with.

"Thank you for bringing me here." I refused to acknowledge the tears that were threatening.

"Babe." He pulled me against his chest. "Thank *you*. It wouldn't be the same without you."

He sounded touched. I still felt close to tears. Thankfully, we heard something behind us. We turned to see a ginormous green lizard stalking the beach. He had talon-like claws, a row of spikes down his back like a mohawk, and a dangling chin like a turkey.

He stopped to inspect us.

"Holy shit!" I screeched. "Is that an iguana?"

"Indeed it is," laughed Cole.

"I'm in love!" I rushed to visit the majestic beast. "I've always wanted to meet an iguana!"

Cole laughed again, then scratched his head. "Jenny, have I ever mentioned that you're one of a kind?"

I MADE friends with the pool bartender. She told me that my new iguana buddy was partial to mangos and beet greens, and she snuck me a secret supply of both. I kept them in my bag and intermittently fed Iggy, as I'd started calling him, under the table.

He'd followed us up from the beach. He could tell I was a sucker for a majestic-looking lizard. He could have been a dinosaur with that spiky ridge on his back!

Cole laughed about it. He kept telling me I was adorable and holding my hand. "I think Iggy's into you," he chided. "It might have something to do with the crop top and the thong bikini."

I grinned. "Or it might be the beet greens."

We had fruity drinks with umbrellas while we sat beside the infinity *pool*. I was feeding an iguana from my secret stash of beet greens. Cole and I were sharing a watermelon and feta salad and an order of truffle fries. I had zero idea what a truffle was, but I knew it wasn't a seared octopus, so it was okay. And the fries were delish!

All this was the long way of saying I was having the time of my life. "Coley, I always wanted to go to an island. But this is so much better than I even dreamed about," I admitted.

He squeezed my hand and gave me one of his looks, deep into my eyes. "This is better than I dreamed about, too."

We smiled at each other, all happy and dopey. That dang weed of hope sprung up inside me again, begging to be tended to, begging for more water and more light. Begging for more of Cole's words. Luckily, Audrey and James entered the bar. Happy for the distraction, I nodded toward them. "They look better. *Way* better."

"Wow, you're right." Cole inspected the much happier-looking couple. "I'm glad to see it."

"You think they're a good couple?" I asked.

"I think they're a great couple." He smiled. "I've never seen James like this with a woman before."

I nodded. Selfishly, I wanted to ask: what about you, Cole? But of course I didn't. This wasn't about me.

Cole waved them over, a grin on his face. "I see some people who look like they had sex and made-up."

"We didn't have sex," James said good-naturedly. But I could see how Cole thought so. James's skin was flushed and glowing, a happy smile on his face.

"You didn't?" Cole asked. He looked impressed. "You might as well put a ring on it, bro. You're done for."

"Cole, leave them alone," I said, punching him playfully. "You two go have lunch and then come swimming with us."

I stood up and grinned at Audrey. "I'm glad you two look happy again." I couldn't wait to hear the details, but I could tell they needed privacy. Iggy the iguana scooted out from beneath the table and booked it toward the beach. I hoped I would see him again later.

We headed toward the pool, and Cole put his hand firmly on my ass. I turned and winked at Audrey before putting my aviator sunglasses on. She had her billionaire, and I had mine.

And even if, for me, it was only for a little while longer, having Cole by my side was wonderful.

It was something. It was everything.

When you vacationed with billionaires, no one worried about how high the bar tab was getting. The older guests, including Mr. and Mrs. Preston, sat under umbrellas, playing cards and sipping an endless supply of white wine. Mrs. Preston intermittently cast disapproving scowls at Audrey, but my friend seemed to be cheerfully ignoring her. She was currently being pinned up against the side of the pool by James. They were seriously making out—she was probably enjoying herself too much to give old Celia any attention.

The rest of us were drinking rum punches punctuated by shots of tequila. Probably not a great combination, but the white-linen-clad waitstaff kept serving them, so... By the time the sun started to set, there were a lot of extremely drunk, extremely rich people around the infinity pool.

All the rum punches were making Cole competitive. Or maybe it was the tequila? In any event, he'd challenged Todd and Evie to a cannonball contest. In between jumps, we were doing tequila shots. Even though Evie and I were competing against each other, we kept giving each other knuckles and high-fives in between rounds. Evie hadn't been my favorite to start with, but now that she was married and all and had invited me on her honeymoon, and we'd had four shots of tequila and endless rum punches, I was starting to warm up to her.

Cole jumped up and did a massive cannonball, leaving an atomic blast of water in his wake. It was clearly the winning splash. "Woo hoo! Yes, babe!" I clapped and jumped up and down on the side of the pool. When Cole came up from underwater, I reached down to give him a high five.

But he pulled me into the pool and gave me a huge kiss.

"This is the best day ever," he said as we floated in a victory lap. "I can't remember the last time I had this much fun."

I grinned at him. I was just drunk enough that the weed of hope was jutting proudly in my chest, and I had zero intentions at the moment of pulling it out. *I could be happy. I AM happy...*

I kissed him, other words floating inside my head. *I love you. I love you, and never have I ever said that to a man.*

It was either cowardice or the tequila that kept me from saying it out loud. Scratch that—it was *definitely* the cowardice.

The tequila had other things to say. "Coley, is it okay to sleep in the pool? And can we bring Iggy back to the casita tonight?" Those were the last things I remember saying before falling asleep (or rather, passing out) in my fake boyfriend's arms.

CHAPTER 28
Cole

"Jenny. *Babe*. I brought you a coffee."

She blearily opened one eye. "Huh?" she croaked.

"Coffee," I enunciated slowly. "You know, the beverage?"

"Oh, that's funny. Ha ha." But she grimaced a little as she sat up. "You'd think I was some novice, mixing rum punches with tequila. I guess I got carried away with all those little umbrellas."

"You aren't the only one." I laughed. "I saw Todd at breakfast. Three of the bridesmaids were throwing up last night."

She rubbed her temples. "You already went to breakfast?"

I nodded. "It's almost noon, so I'm waking you up. I knew you wouldn't want to miss the day."

"It's that late?" She sounded distressed. "I don't want to miss a minute of our vacation! Let me go and get dressed—"

I gently grabbed her wrist. "Easy, girl. There's no rush. There's plenty of time left this week. And I'm sure there'll be more Caribbean vacations in your future."

There was an awkward silence, and Jenny winced. But she recovered so quickly, I might've imagined it.

"I'm going to take a quick shower and get dressed," she said swiftly. "Then we can go out and do whatever you want."

I watched her face. It was a smooth, impenetrable mask. *Fuck*. I'd just said the wrong thing, and I knew it.

This might be Jenny's first and only trip to the Caribbean. The things I took for granted—like the inevitably of another luxury vacation—were by no means guaranteed in Jenny's world.

"How about some lunch, a beach walk, and then swimming?" I asked, trying to make it right. "Maybe we can find Iggy and feed him a snack?"

"Sounds perfect." She gave me a bright smile that didn't quite reach her eyes and then hustled to the bathroom. I heard her turn the shower on, and I lay back in bed, cursing myself.

I'm sure there'll be more Caribbean vacations in your future.

I really was an insensitive ass sometimes. First of all, we were currently on a romantic vacation *together*. And yet, I'd said "your future" to her, not "our future." Second, who was I to assume that Jenny would ever take another vacation like this? If we weren't together, what would happen to her once we returned to Boston?

That was the question that had kept me awake as I'd tossed and turned all night. I'd awoken this morning with no answer. I'd also apparently awoken with no tact. I'd hurt Jenny's feelings, and it had been entirely inadvertent. *Way to go, Cole.*

Jenny and the bridesmaids weren't the only ones to suffer from the rum punches and tequila shots. I hadn't slept much due to the combination of alcohol and my swirling thoughts. Day one of our vacation had been great —one of the best days ever. But it had left me unsettled. Why would I want our arrangement to end if I was having so much fun and feeling happy?

The truth was, I didn't want to say goodbye to Jenny when we got back home. I couldn't even imagine it. But what else could I do? We were from two different worlds. And I'd only known her for a week. When I hired her as my fake date, I had zero intention of getting attached. Given my relationship track record, I hadn't even considered it a possibility. And now I had my father to think about, my inheritance, my empire...

I stared up at the ceiling, remembering the idea I'd had—the one about having a *kept woman*. The term was antiquated, misogynistic, and disparaging. It also had an undeniable appeal. I could keep Jenny safe, and more importantly, I could keep her just for me. No other man was going to touch her. I could set her up in a condominium, ensure she had everything she needed, and maybe things could stay the way they were between us. No one had to know about my private life, not even my father: that's why it was called *private*.

What would Jenny say about any of this? I had no idea. I'd been too chicken to raise the topic of the future with her. Whenever I thought about bringing it up, an unfamiliar and uncomfortable feeling swept through me—self-doubt. What if she wasn't interested in pursuing our relationship? What if she wanted nothing to do with me? What if she was faking?

I lay there, considering the uncomfortable questions circling in my mind. Then, I had an answer: *nah*. First of all, women, in general, loved me. They always had. I was handsome, muscular, rich AF, and great in bed. That was just the truth, and I knew it.

Second, Jenny herself liked me. I knew she did. I made her laugh, and she wasn't faking. Our sex was electric—and she wasn't faking that, either. I believed she was genuinely having a good time with me. And I had as much fun being at a fancy dinner with her as I did walking down the street. All of it was good. Being close to each other seemed natural for both of us. I'd woken up that morning holding her hand. The affection between us wasn't my imagination; it was real.

I just didn't know what to do with it.

A few minutes later, Jenny came out of the bathroom. Her curls were still damp, and her face was bare of makeup. She looked more beautiful to me than ever.

"I'm almost ready," she said. "Are you wearing your bathing suit to lunch, or do we come back to change? All this resort stuff is new to me." Jenny still sounded slightly off, and I knew I'd hurt her.

"You can wear your suit and a cover-up. We can leave right from lunch to walk the beach. I'll pack a bag with sunscreen and waters. And some mango. And beet greens." I would literally do anything to make it up to her. "Okay, babe?"

"Okay." She smiled, but again, it seemed forced.

I sighed. "Can you come here for a second?"

"Sure." She came and obediently sat on the edge of the bed.

"I'm sorry if I hurt your feelings just now."

Her eyeballs almost popped out of her head. "Why do you think you hurt my feelings?"

"Because I could see it on your face," I said.

"Oh." Jenny touched her cheek as though it might have some explaining to do. "Sorry."

"Why are you saying sorry?"

"I didn't think you could tell." She shrugged. "I didn't mean to make a big deal out of nothin'."

"You didn't make a big deal, and you certainly don't need to apologize." I hesitated before I said more, mostly because I didn't know what to say. "I kind of suck at this," I explained.

She blinked. "At what?"

"Talking about...things."

She nodded. "Me too. But we don't need to talk about things, right?" she asked anxiously. "We can just get lunch, walk the beach, and swim."

"Right." I reached out and took her hands. "But I've been thinking..."

Jenny tensed. We really were alike. She seemed to be dreading this conversation as much as I was.

I took a deep breath. "Jenny, what would you say if I told you I don't want you to go back to working for the agency when we get home?"

"Um..." She bit her lip. "I get it. I mean, I think I get it?"

"I want us to be exclusive," I said quickly.

"I see." She frowned, which was not the reaction I was hoping for.

"You don't want to be exclusive?" I held my breath.

"It's not that," she said immediately. "It's just...I can't make rent working at Sizzler, you know?"

"Right—I know. I was thinking that maybe you wouldn't have to work. Or that you wouldn't have to pay rent. Or something." I scrubbed a hand across my face.

Jenny didn't save me from myself. She sat there, waiting for me to go on. I felt myself break into a cold sweat.

"What would you like to see happen when we get back?" I asked, coward that I was. Now, the ball was in her court.

She opened her mouth and then closed it. "I... I don't know."

Her tone was making me feel insecure—a foreign, unwelcome sensation. But Jenny was smart. If I wasn't going to show her mine, she wasn't about to show me hers. She was waiting for me to put my cards on the table so she could adjust accordingly.

Although I sucked at relationships, I was good at negotiating deals. So I snapped out of my panic long enough to remember the rules: listen more than talk, and never make the first offer if you could avoid it. I had to get something, anything, from Jenny. Then, I'd have a place to start.

"That's fair. I know I'm being a little broad." I

nodded. "How about I ask you a couple of questions, and you can answer yes or no?"

"Okay." But she sounded wary.

"Do you want to return to AccommoDating when the trip ends?" I asked.

She shrugged. "Not necessarily."

"Would you... Jenny, would you like to live in a different apartment? Someplace nice?"

She waited for a moment. Then she smiled at me, but it wasn't "my" Jenny's smile. It was a smile I'd seen before. Mostly from parties on the other side of a business deal when they had zero intention of playing by my rules. "Coley, why don't you just say what you want to say? You're askin' me all these questions, but like you said, it's too 'broad.' I don't know what you want."

I sighed. "I don't know what *you* want."

"Then I guess we're even." She eyed me appraisingly.

"I guess you did say some things you want—or don't want. You said you don't want me hooking anymore." Jenny's tone was matter-of-fact. "And you don't want me working at Sizzler. So it sounds like you've *some* ideas."

"I'd like to hear your ideas first," I said plaintively.

"Ha Coley, okay. Here's my idea: how about you make me an offer I can't refuse." Her eyes sparkled. She knew she had me. "And I will entertain it."

"You know what, Jenny?"

She arched an eyebrow. "What?"

"You're smart."

"I know," she said. "It's my secret weapon."

I sighed again. "Here's an offer you can't refuse. How about I buy you an apartment, huh?"

She didn't look as excited as I'd hoped.

"And any kind of car you want? What did you say you liked—Range Rovers? How about I buy you a South End condo and a Range Rover?" I asked somewhat desperately.

She smiled at me, but again, it wasn't with the exuberance I'd expected. "That sounds real good, Coley," she said. "A South End condo and a Range Rover is an offer a girl like me sure can't refuse."

"So, are you *accepting* my offer?"

Jenny kept smiling. "Yes, Coley. I am accepting it. How about we go down to the beach and find Iggy to celebrate? I still have some of those mustard greens in my bag!"

She bent and gave me a quick kiss, then hustled to go and get ready.

And I just sat there, feeling a little sick. I knew I'd somehow blown a crucial negotiation, even though I'd gotten everything on my list.

She'd said yes.

She wasn't going back to hooking—we'd be exclusive.

She was going to live in the South End condo I'd buy for her.

She was going to drive the Range Rover I'd give her as a gift.

She'd said it was a great offer. An offer she couldn't refuse.

And yet, even though she'd agreed to all of it, it didn't feel like a win.

I'd lost something, and I wasn't even sure what it was.

CHAPTER 29
Jenny

WE MADE IT THROUGH THE DAY MOSTLY unscathed. And by unscathed, I meant that Cole and I had enjoyed the resort. We swam in the gorgeous water, made love, ate delicious food, fed Iggy the Iguana, remembered to apply sunscreen and hydrate regularly, and hadn't talked further about Things That Made Me Upset.

So, I was *mostly* unscathed by the time we sat down for dinner with the whole wedding crew. We were in an outdoor seating area with tiki torches and candles, with a view of the ocean and the stars above. It was amazing, and I vowed to enjoy myself. I should be happy. After all, I was unscathed by Cole's offer of a South End condo and a Range Rover.

Mostly.

"I'd like to make a toast," Todd said and stood. "First

of all, to Evie for agreeing to marry me. I would have been in sad shape if she'd said no." He leaned down and kissed her, and everybody whooped and clapped.

"Second, I'd like to thank my parents and Evie's parents for hosting such a beautiful wedding celebration. It was perfect in every way. Thank you for organizing and for, well, paying." Everyone laughed.

"Third, I'd like to thank my brother James for being my best man, and for taking time out of his busy schedule to actually go on vacation for once. I have a feeling I should really be thanking his girlfriend, Audrey, since James has never been this relaxed in his life. So cheers to James and Audrey. And cheers to all of you for joining us on this happy occasion. To the hair of the dog!" Todd said and knocked back his shot.

"The hair of the dog." Everyone clinked glasses and drank their tequila, me included. But the shot didn't make me feel any better. I was happy for Todd and Evie—I swear to God I was—but hearing about their happiness, happy occasion, fabulous vacation with their parents and friends, and legitimate happily-ever-after was sort of making me unhappy. It was sort of making me want to puke.

I leaned over to Audrey, who I hadn't had a chance to talk to all day. "Can we take a break?" I asked.

"Sure," she said.

I grabbed her hand, and we walked from the oceanside restaurant to the central part of the resort. "I just need a little space," I said, looking back at the table. Cole was talking to Todd and James.

"Is everything okay?" Audrey asked.

I could feel the hurt bubbling up inside me. I'd kept it in all day, but there was no avoiding it now. I shook my head. "No. No, it is not."

We found a private bathroom with a lounge area; we went inside and locked the door. I started pacing, unsure what to say. My thoughts and feelings were all jumbled up, making me emotional. I didn't like feeling that way. I wanted that piece of me that was always in control to come back, save me from myself, and make the threatening tears take a hike and never return.

"What's wrong?" Audrey asked.

"It's Cole," I said. "He told me he doesn't want me to go back to work after this. He said he wants me to be exclusive."

All of a sudden, the tears were winning. I headed for the vanity and checked my makeup, ensuring my mascara stayed intact.

"Is that a bad thing?" she asked. "You don't want to be exclusive?"

"It's not that," I said. I gritted my teeth and then examined them for lipstick. "It's that he said he'd buy me an apartment, buy me whatever kind of car I wanted, blah blah blah."

"Oh. Huh." Audrey sounded confused. "And that's bad?"

"Yeah, it's bad, Dre," I said. "'Cause that's not what I want!"

Audrey was watching me carefully. "What *do* you want?"

"More." I rolled my eyes at myself in the mirror. "Jesus, you'd think I was some kind of amateur. I shoulda never come on this trip."

Audrey came closer and rubbed my arm. "It's okay, Jenny. But did you tell him how you felt?"

I snorted. "No fucking way. He told me he didn't want me to go back to hooking after this trip. So I told him to make me an offer I couldn't refuse, ya know? And he made me an offer I couldn't refuse. It was just the wrong one."

"I think you should talk to him," she said. "Just like you told me to talk to James. Remember? When you told me to be brave?"

"I'm not you, Dre. It's not possible to clean this up," I said, motioning to myself, "put it into a Volvo, and pretend it knows how to play tennis. Do you understand?"

Audrey nodded while I got back to carefully blotting my eyes. "I don't know if Cole cares about Volvos and tennis, Jenny," she said. "But I'm pretty sure he cares about you."

"Do not try to turn my airplane pep talk around on me," I said. Now I felt like I might really start bawling. "This is totally different."

"If you say so," Audrey said. She didn't sound like she meant it. "But you had some pretty good advice. I'm just saying."

I blew out a deep breath. "What about you and James?" I asked, changing the subject. "You looked a lot happier in the pool earlier. Are you all better?"

She nodded. "He asked me to move to California with him."

"I knew it!" I cried. "I knew it! I could tell just by looking at him. You're gonna live happily ever after."

"I don't know about that," she said.

"I do." I looked at her levelly. "I *know* it's gonna happen."

She met my gaze. "Jenny, I see the way Cole is with you. I think he's in love with you."

"I thought he was, too," I said, returning to my reflection and fluffing my hair. "But it must have just been that thing with his balls. I do it exactly the way he likes."

I smiled at Audrey in the mirror. "I'm not even mad at him, though. He's great. I'm mad at *me*. I think I got too inspired by my own pep talk. I'm the one who started hoping—and that was a dumb fucking move. If I hadn't hoped, I'd be psyched that I was getting a South End condo and a Range Rover. Now all I'm doing is crying." I blew my nose.

"You should give him a chance," she said. "See what he has to say for himself."

"I'll think about it," I said and gave my hair one final fluff. "In the meantime, I need some liquid courage to keep up with these people. Rich people sure drink a lot, huh?"

We headed back to the restaurant. Unfortunately, Celia Preston waited in the hallway. Celia was an attractive woman, well-preserved by facial fillers, plastic surgery, and what I assumed was the ice running through her veins. But the constant sneer on her face contorted her good looks, twisting her.

I shivered, remembering what Celia had said about James's dead girlfriend. *You dodged a bullet.* Who said shit like that?

"May I have a word with you, Audrey?" Celia asked. She looked at me pointedly. "Alone?"

"Of course, Mrs. Preston," Audrey mumbled.

Despite Celia's warning glare, I didn't budge from Audrey's side. "You okay?" I asked her, keeping my voice low.

"It'll be okay," she whispered. "I hope."

"If you don't come back in five minutes, I'll be back with reinforcements." I squeezed her hand and then headed back to the restaurant.

"Where's Audrey?" James asked as I sat down.

"She's talking to your mom."

He arched an eyebrow.

"If she's not back in five minutes, let's go get her," I said.

"Deal." James sat, shoulders tensed, as he watched the door.

We didn't have to wait long—Audrey and Celia returned, taking their respective seats without a word. But Audrey looked pale, her mouth set in a grim line. James leaned over and talked to her, and then they got up to leave.

"She's not feeling well," he explained.

"I bet." I watched as Audrey straightened her shoulders and left the restaurant, head held high. My friend had been through a lot in her life. Whatever the hell Celia Preston had just said to her, Audrey had most likely been through worse.

I hoped.

"Everything okay?" Cole asked me.

Celia Preston watched me from the head of the table. Her icy, shrewd gaze missed nothing.

"I hope so," I said.

CHAPTER 30
Cole

THE NEXT MORNING, JENNY WAS IN THE SHOWER, singing an upbeat Taylor Swift song. I took it as a good sign. We'd enjoyed the rest of the day yesterday. Jenny had still seemed slightly off, but she was mostly fine.

Until we'd gone to bed that night. She hadn't been one hundred percent her usual self. We'd made love. I'd still orgasmed, she'd still orgasmed, but... She hadn't done that thing with my balls. And she *always* did it. She knew I loved it. Maybe she just wanted to mix things up...?

But if it wasn't broke, why fix it? Our sex made me feel that I was correct, that Jenny was not being herself.

Still, as the new day dawned, I felt less worried about my sack and more optimistic about our proposed arrangement. The fact that she was singing a happy pop song helped. Not to mention that a South End condo and a Range Rover were objectively a pretty sweet deal. Not that I cared about the material components—I cared about *her* and keeping her safe. Our tentative agreement would do that and more.

It would also keep her in my life until I found a way to...keep her in my life.

My phone pinged with two texts from Kevin. I didn't mean to read them, but the words caught my eye, delivering the blow of bad news.

> He's hired a private detective to investigate the girl.

> I'll probably get fired for telling you that.

Fuck. Nice move, Dad.

I deleted the messages. There was nothing I could do while we were away. But then I sat there, ruminating, wondering how the hell I would handle this situation. Because it *was* a situation, now. My father was like a dog with a bone. Once he got his teeth into something, he wouldn't stop until he ripped it to shreds.

I argued with myself, examining both sides. On the one hand, he was threatening Jenny by hiring someone to look into her. There was no outright danger at the moment, but that could change at any time. I needed to protect her from his ire. Hopefully, getting her out of the business would help shield her. If she were holed up in her South End condo, she would be that much more removed from the heat of any fires he started.

On the other hand, I wondered if I was overthinking the whole thing. So what if my father hired an investigator? Jenny was an escort. I knew that, my father knew that, and Jenny knew that. I wasn't sure what he was thinking, trying to dig up more dirt.

If this was more ammunition for him to threaten me about my inheritance, so be it. My father was an ass, but he was also proud. Surely he wouldn't squander his vast fortune. He'd spent a lifetime amassing his wealth. He wouldn't *actually* disinherit me and give the money to strangers who also happened to be low-lying fruit enemies of mine.

He was vindictive, but he wasn't reckless.

I decided, once again, that all of this was his problem. Not mine. And I refused to think about my father or the private investigator for another minute while on vacation. There was nothing I could do from the island except let it be. In fact, we were heading out on a snorkeling excursion with Todd, Evie, James, Audrey, and some of the others; I would be happy to put some distance between myself and my phone right now.

Jenny looked super-hot in yet another thong bikini

and a sexy cover-up. She grinned at me when I said, "I'm going to have to give Shirley a raise."

"You totally should," she agreed. "Wait till I show you the lingerie she bought me!"

I felt relieved—Jenny seemed much more like herself. We packed sunscreen, water, and mango for her new iguana BFF, then headed down to the beach. Jenny put me at ease, chatting and ooh-ing and aah-ing over the resort and the island. She was like a kid at Disneyland, happy and carefree. What had I been so worried about?

When we reached the dock, she made a beeline for Audrey. James took the opportunity to pull me aside. "How's it going with Jenny?"

"Awesome. She's incredible. I've never met anyone like her," I said.

James raised his eyebrows. "Are you talking about her in a sexual way? Or as a person?"

I gave him a long look. "I didn't realize it was necessary to parse this out," I said. "But I meant both."

"What's going to happen after this trip?" he asked.

"What's going to happen with you and Audrey?" I countered. "I asked you first, if you'll remember. Back in Boston."

"I asked her to move to California with me," he said. "I love her."

I almost fell off the dock. "To borrow Jenny's phrase: Ho my frickin' God, James. I'm so proud of you." I clapped him on the back and grinned. "I knew it."

"Well, you were right," he said, grinning back. "Now I want to know if I'm right about you."

"Huh," I said. "This should be interesting." I was half-excited, half-dreading his assessment.

"I think you have real feelings for this girl," James said. "I think you might just have an emotional boner for her."

I sighed. Then I nodded. "It's obvious, right? It's *big*."

"It's not as big as mine, but you can still see it," he joked.

"Ha," I said. I watched Jenny as she laughed and talked to Audrey.

"I think I might be in love with her," I admitted. My jaw clenched as I said it—maybe I was trying to keep the words from getting out. Because once they were out, they were real.

"She told Audrey you offered to buy her a house when we get back," James said.

"That's right." I nodded. "I asked her what she wanted, and she told me she wanted a South End condo and a Range Rover. So I said done and done."

"What if that's not all she wants?"

"What do you mean?" I asked, confused.

"What if she wants you to be her boyfriend?"

"I frickin' hope she wants me to be her boyfriend if I'm buying her a South End condo and a Range Rover." I looked at him, still confused. "Is she upset or something? She wouldn't even do that thing with my balls last night."

"Cole, please—"

"No, but she always does it. And I didn't know what was wrong. She wouldn't tell me. And she's not usually like that. She's always open with me. And I mean *really* open—"

"Stop," he said, holding up his hands in mock surrender. "Please, *please* spare me the details. All I know is that she told Audrey what you offered her and that she wants more."

"More than a condo and a car?"

"Yes, Cole."

"Like what?" I asked, thoroughly perplexed.

"Like *you*. In the condo and in the car."

"I was planning on being in the condo and in the car," I said. "That's sort of the point."

"You should tell her," he said. "Just be really clear. Sometimes they need to hear it with an exclamation point."

"Sounds like you, bro." I smiled at James.

Historically, James was even more emotionally unintelligent than me. But he seemed to be making a pretty decent point. Even though he was a prick, he was my best friend for a reason.

And that's because he was, indeed, the best.

WE SNORKELED ALL MORNING, which was fun. Jenny went wild over all the colorful fish—she was the first one in the water and the last one out. Then, our party headed back to the beach for a break.

Jenny and I took the opportunity to go for a romantic walk. I'd learned she enjoyed walking the beach, picking up shells, and splashing in the water as we roamed. I could walk a thousand miles with her. She smiled at the water, the sun, and anyone we passed. She seemed happy and content—but after what James had told me, I wondered if that had to do more with our surroundings than with me.

I laced my fingers through hers and didn't say anything for a few minutes. I'd had enough time for James's words to sink in. I'd also had time to process that my father was on the warpath and that I'd have to deal with him when I got home. I didn't want Jenny to be collateral damage in his game. I had to protect her. When we returned to Boston, I would have to face my father and have it out with him once and for all.

But that was then. This was now.

"Coley," she said, "I feel like I need to talk to you about something."

I nodded. "Me too."

"Yeah? Okay…" She glanced at me. "Can you go first?"

I chuckled. "I guess so."

I'd been a coward yesterday. Today, it was time to be a man.

The man she deserved.

"I agree—we should talk." I stopped walking, but I didn't stop holding her hand. "I need to tell you something."

She perched her sunglasses on top of her head. The easy, sunny smile was gone, replaced by a worried expression. She straightened her shoulders and looked me in the eye. She took a deep breath, seeming to gather her courage. "S'okay, Cole. Go ahead. Just say it."

"I love you."

She blinked at me like maybe I hadn't said it in English. An uncomfortable silence stretched between us, broken only by the surf crashing against the shore.

Jenny didn't take her eyes off my face. "You… You *love* me?"

I nodded. Had there been some way to backtrack out of the statement, I surely would have. I had never said that to a woman in my life—except for my mom, of course, but that was different. It was also a lifetime ago. I felt petrified, standing there. Only fools put all their cards on the table and hoped for the best. I knew better.

I knew better, but I'd still done it.

Jenny clutched my hands. "Cole, I... I..."

My heart sank. "It's okay, Jenny. Go ahead," I said, taking a page from her playbook. "Just say it."

"I love you, too." Her eyes filled with tears.

"You *do*?"

"'Course I do," she said, blotting her eyes. "But I ain't never said that to anybody before, and *ho my God*, I just said 'ain't'—that's an old bad habit, and I *never* thought I would say it to anybody—I love you, not ain't—and I *never* thought I would say it to *you*, or that you would say it to *me*—"

"Jenny," I interrupted, "can I kiss you now? So maybe we can both stop talking?"

"Good idea." She leaned forward and put her lips to mine, and the easy heat ignited between us. I delved my hands into her long, damp curls, and she collided with my chest. My hands were everywhere, her hands were everywhere, and we were in love.

We broke apart, both breathing hard.

"Ho my frickin' God," I said, crying and laughing. "I love you."

"That makes two of us, Coley." Jenny beamed at me, even as her eyes shone with tears. "And I can't believe it. I'm the luckiest girl in the whole world. I'm in the Caribbean and I'm in love. How lucky is that?"

"It's lucky," I agreed, holding her close. I inhaled her coconut-y scent. "It's pretty freaking lucky."

CHAPTER 31
Jenny

WE RETURNED TO THE BOAT AND SNORKELED ALL afternoon, laughing, talking, and enjoying the beautiful surroundings. Cole and I were in love: it was official. The water seemed more turquoise, the sun seemed to shine brighter, and the tropical fish seemed more tropical.

It was the best day of my life.

I'd been *dying* to talk to Audrey and find out what had happened with Celia Preston. We hadn't had a chance to be alone all day, but when everyone else was in the water, and the captain was out of earshot, we finally got to talk.

"What happened with Mrs. Voldemort last night?" I asked.

Audrey shuddered. "It was bad. She hired a private investigator to find out about me, Jenny! She knows that I'm an escort. She knows about you, too."

Oh fuck. This wasn't good news. I didn't care that Mrs. Preston knew about me, but Audrey was another matter. "She's the devil!" I said, crossing myself. "I can't stand to be in the same room with her. What'd she say?"

"She threatened me and offered to pay me off to go away—right after she called me a whore," Audrey said as she stared out at the water. "You know. Pretty much what you'd expect."

"That bitch!" I snorted. "Did you tell James?"

"I did. He's furious," she said. "He told her this morning that I'm moving in with him and that he loves me."

"Yes, James!" I fist-pumped. "I'm officially rooting for him."

A smile broke through Audrey's tense expression. "Thank you, Jenny. That means a lot. I love him."

"I love that he stood up for you. That's the way it should be." I beamed at my friend. "What'd Celia say?"

"Not too much. I don't think she wanted to make him any angrier," she said. "But just watch out for her. She's a barracuda."

"I can handle her." I tossed my curls. "It's just too bad I can't use a spear gun on her bony ass."

"I wish you could, too," Audrey sighed. "She's honestly scary. But it seems like James handled her well this morning. I don't know what's going to happen next, but..."

"I do." I grinned at my friend. "You and James are going to live happily ever after. No matter what that bitch says!"

"Ha. I hope so. But speaking of happily ever after... Are things better with you and Cole?" she asked. "You two seem like you're being very romantic."

She'd probably noticed that we'd been holding hands, kissing, and making goo-goo eyes at each other since our walk.

"I decided to talk to him. Like you said." I took my sunglasses off and stuck them on my hat. I wanted my friend to see how truly happy I was.

"Being brave was *your* idea if I remember correctly," she said.

"That's right—'cause I'm so wicked smart," I said and laughed. "He told me he loved me just now, Dre. He said he wants to move in with me when we get back."

"That's so awesome!" Audrey's eyes filled with tears.

"It is pretty frickin' awesome," I agreed. "We can double date, and it'll be box seats all the way, baby."

"It's crazy, right?" she asked. "Who'd have thought?"

"Me," I said proudly. "This is where I get to say I told you so!"

"You did," Audrey admitted, then sighed.

Cole and I talked that night about what happened with Celia Preston. He agreed—James's mother was a barracuda, stealthy and dangerous. "Stay away from her for the rest of the trip," he warned.

I wholeheartedly agreed. "You don't have to tell me twice! Bitch scares me!"

I was so happy in my little casita later that afternoon with Cole. Now that we'd declared our feelings, we could luxuriate in being together. So we did our usual things—made love twice and ate snacks. You couldn't beat it! I also left out little fruit tidbits for the birds and the lizards. We spent an hour sitting side by side, watching the wildlife enjoy their treats.

If there was a heaven, it just might be the Caribbean.

"We should come back here every year," Cole mused. "All of us."

The fact that he was talking about us in the future didn't escape my attention. I grinned at him. "You don't have to ask me twice," I said. "I'm in!"

But things got a little crazy at dinner. We were all eating at the outdoor restaurant again when Audrey and James showed up. We'd had such an awesome day snorkeling, but now they both looked stressed. They sat down next to James's parents, which I thought was odd, given

Audrey's conversation with Celia Preston the night before.

What was even more bizarre? After dinner, James and Audrey led his parents out to the foyer.

And then they...left. I didn't see them for the rest of the night, and I didn't get any texts from Audrey.

The next morning, Todd told us they'd left the island.

"What do you mean, they *left*?" Cole asked Todd.

Todd raked a hand through his hair. "My mother said James and Audrey had some sort of a blowout. James was bringing her back to Boston."

"That's crazy." Cole scowled at him. "They were having a great time yesterday."

"I know." Todd shook his head. "Something doesn't seem right. But maybe they just had a fight and wanted to be alone. It happens."

I checked my phone all day. I didn't hear a word from Audrey; Cole didn't hear from James.

"I don't know, Coley. Something about this really seems off. They've been on the love boat ever since the wedding. She just agreed to move to California with him. And Dre isn't the type to have some silly fight," I said.

"I know." Cole looked thoughtful. "It doesn't make sense."

"Something seems fishy," I agreed. "I guess we'll hear about it when we get back."

"Speaking of when we get back." Cole turned to me. "Would you do me a favor?"

"Anything," I cooed.

He picked up my phone and handed it to me. "Would you call Elena and quit? I want to make it official."

I winked at him. "I'll call her, don't worry. And then we'll be officially official."

"I like the way that sounds, Jenny." He took my hand, sat back and relaxed. "I really like the way that sounds."

"Elena, don't get mad at me, okay?" I clutched the phone.

"Mad at you for what? Don't tell me you ran out on our billionaire client!" she wailed.

"Nah, it's nothing like that." I took a deep breath. "The thing is, Cole wants to *buy* me. He's getting me a South End Condo and a Range Rover. He wants to be exclusive, Elena. No more Fat Vinnie or Loopsy!"

"Wow, Jenny..." The silence stretched out as Elena processed the news. "I'm really happy to hear that."

"You are?" I scratched my head. "I thought you'd be pissed!"

"Absolutely not. I'm a CEO, so for me it's always business first," the Madam explained. "But every once in a while I get to see a happy ending for one of my girls, and it's satisfying. You deserve the best, Jenny. I'm glad that Mr. Bryson can see that."

My eyes filled with tears. I hadn't expected this kind of response from her. "That's real nice, Elena." I reached for a tissue and blow-honked my nose. "It means a lot."

"Tell Mr. Bryson to send me his friends," she said, switching back to CEO-mode. "You know I'm always looking for referrals!"

WE DIDN'T HEAR anything from James or Audrey for the next two days. Worrying about them made the rest of our vacation less fun, but it made packing up and getting on the return flight easier.

When it was time to go, I kissed Iggy the iguana goodbye, which Cole thought was totally gross. "He's like my adopted baby," I argued, giving the giant iguana one final beet green. "I'm going to miss him."

What I *wasn't* going to miss was Celia Preston. Since Audrey had left, she'd been busy focusing her evil eye on me. In response, I wore only thong bikinis all day, every day, including to meals. Old Celia's evil eye was getting an eyeful, all right!

The flight home was quick, but my nerves were jumpy.

What would it be like being back in Boston with Cole as my plus-one? What would it be like to live in a fancy apartment and not have to "date" Johns to make rent? To not have to struggle? What the heck was I going to *do*? I had zero idea.

Still, I was excited as we landed at Logan and entered the terminal. Boston wasn't as gorgeous and sunny as the Caribbean, but the gray skyline and puffy white clouds were still home.

Todd and Evie were the first ones off the plane, followed by us. I couldn't believe it—James and Audrey were waiting in the terminal.

"Yay!" I said to Cole, squeezing his hand. "Look who's here!"

Todd reached them first. James grabbed his shoulders and appeared to be talking to him about something real important, judging by the look on his face. Audrey stood beside them, listening intently, her face drawn.

James motioned to an older couple standing behind them, and then Todd shook their hands.

"What the heck's going on?" I asked Cole. "Who're those people?'

"I don't know—let's go see." He hustled me closer, and we just caught the end of James and Todd's conversation.

"Mother has been implicated in Danielle's death,"

James was saying. "She threatened Audrey, and we started putting the pieces together. The police are here to bring her in for questioning, and maybe Dad, too. And Danielle's parents are here to see them face-to-face." He motioned to the older couple standing behind them.

Cole and I looked at each other, gobsmacked.

"Holy shit," Cole said under his breath. "The *police*?"

Todd went white. "Are you kidding?" he asked James.

"No. I'm sorry, I'm not," James said. "It happened so long ago, but Mother needs to be held responsible for what she did."

"I'm so sorry," Todd said. "I had no idea."

"Me either." James clapped Todd on the shoulder. "We'll get through this. I'm sorry to drop it on you."

"It's okay." But Todd looked pale.

Evie put her arm around her husband. "Come and sit down," Evie said, her voice gentle. She led Todd to a nearby seat, talking to him softly and rubbing his arm.

Todd looked like he was in shock, and I didn't blame him. *James's mom was responsible for Danielle's death?*

She was being *arrested*?

"Holy wow," I said as I reached James and Audrey. "Are you guys okay?"

Audrey pulled me in for a hug. "I'm so sorry I didn't tell you I was leaving the island," she said. "But we were trying to convince Celia that we were breaking up. We needed a cover—we had to come back to Boston to talk to Danielle's parents and meet with the police."

"I can't believe it. Celia killed James's girlfriend?" I asked, careful to keep my voice low.

"Not exactly." Audrey grimaced. "We think she might have paid someone."

"I'd say I didn't believe it if Mrs. Preston wasn't such a c-word." I shivered. "She just kept looking at me the whole flight, like I was going to infect her with hooker cooties or something."

Audrey gave me an exhausted smile. "I'd say I was surprised, but—"

"Ho my frickin' God, Audrey!" I excitedly whispered, interrupting her. There was something very huge and very sparkly on her left ring finger. "Is that an engagement ring?"

Audrey nodded, and I grabbed her, squeezing hard. I wanted to holler and jump up and down, but being that James's mother was about to be arrested for murder, it didn't seem appropriate.

So instead, I whispered, "It's not even a rock! It's a frickin' *boulder*!"

"Jenny," Audrey said calmly, "let's talk about it later. We have some bad stuff to take care of right now."

"Right," I said. I stopped squeezing Audrey. "But wow. Just wow."

James's mother swept off the plane in a green polo shirt with the collar turned up, immaculate khakis, and white loafers. Beneath the Botox, her face managed to move enough to register shock when she saw James and Audrey.

"James?" she said. "*Audrey?*" She stopped dead in her tracks, Mr. Preston bumping into her from behind. "Watch it, Robert," she snapped.

"Mother, be polite—we have company," James said, motioning to the Andersons. "You remember Mr. and Mrs. Anderson, right? Danielle's parents? And this is Detective Gordon and Detective Fisk from the Boston Police Department. I believe they'd like to ask you and Dad some questions—downtown."

Celia Preston looked confused, then pissed, then outraged as several photographers sprung out and started snapping pictures, their flashes going off.

"And that's the *Tribune*. And the paparazzi." James smiled tightly at her. James said a few other things, mainly about Audrey's mom, but I was so overwhelmed by all the photographers and the look of hatred on Celia's face I missed them.

"Oh—and one more thing," James said. "Audrey and I are engaged."

"Mr. Preston! You're engaged?" called one of the photographers, whizzing around and aiming his huge lens at James and Audrey. "Let me take a shot of the happy couple!"

I stopped myself from cheering, it being an otherwise solemn occasion and all. But inside, I was clapping and jumping up and down. *Sometimes,* I thought, *the good guys actually win.*

"Let's get out of here," Cole said. He put his arm protectively around me as he steered us away from the crowd. I slapped Audrey a surreptitious high five on the way out. *I told you so,* I mouthed.

She managed a smile at me. She knew I was right—I was *always* right. It was another one of my secret weapons. I'd said Celia Preston was Mrs. Voldemort and it was true. I'd *also* said James and Audrey were going to live happily ever after together and that was true, too.

Now, I just had to see if I was right about me.

I glanced up at Cole, and he smiled at me.

I smiled back.

Sometimes, I thought again, *the good guys actually win.*

CHAPTER 32
Cole

"I can't believe it," I told Jenny on the ride home. "I'm not even sure I understand everything yet. But James said his mother was involved in the death of a woman he dated in college. That was before we became friends, but I remember hearing about her—her name was Danielle. She got into a fatal car accident. It was terrible."

"Oh my God." Jenny looked like she might cry. "That's so freaking *terrible*."

We were exhausted after dealing with the fallout from Celia Preston's arrest. As we navigated the short drive from Logan to the Liberty, I was happy to be heading home and away from the terrible scene. I'd known that Celia Preston was a terrible person, but I didn't think she was actually a *terrible person*. Apparently, I'd been wrong.

Amari waited for us at the door, and I was grateful to

see him. "Hi, Mr. Preston, Ms. Jenny. It's nice to have you back," he said.

"Good to see you, Amari. We're glad to be home—long flight," I explained as we emerged from the Porsche, both of us pale beneath our tans and slightly off-kilter. "With a little family drama thrown in for flair."

He nodded at me as he grabbed our bags. "Speaking of family drama," he kept his voice low so Jenny couldn't hear, "there's been somebody sniffing around here. Asking questions about you and Ms. Jenny. They offered me money to talk and to let them up into your place—I didn't do it," he said immediately.

"Fuck," I groaned. "But thank you for letting me know. You're a good guy."

"Do you think it was the Windsor sisters?" he asked. "Do you think they hired someone?"

"Could be." I scrubbed a hand across my face. "But honestly, I've got some other enemies at the moment."

"I'm sorry to spring it on you first thing," he said apologetically. "But I wanted you to know."

"I appreciate that." I made a mental note to either hire Amari away or pressure the manager into giving him a six-figure raise; I wasn't sure which.

Jenny and I dragged ourselves into the lobby, only to be accosted by the Windsor sisters. *FFS*. Greta and

Florence sprung out at us, as though they'd been lying in wait.

"Cole? We've been waiting for you!"

"I don't have time for this right now—"

But they wouldn't take no for an answer. The sisters fired off a machine-gun round of questions so quickly that I couldn't tell who was asking what.

"You were with Celia Preston when she got arrested?"

"She is *such* a bitch! She tried to get me thrown off the board at Children's Hospital! Did she do it? Did she kill that girl?"

"I *knew* she would do something like murder! Did you know the girl who died?"

"Who is James Preston's fiancée? I didn't know he was your best friend. Wait, is he your best friend?"

"Woah—ladies, just *woah*." I gripped Jenny's hand. She looked at the sisters with mild shock. Florence and Greta were an awful lot to handle after a long day.

"First of all," I continued, "I thought you weren't speaking to us. I thought you were getting me thrown out."

Greta pulled her glasses down her nose. "John called us. He said you wanted to buy out our apartment, and it's going to be profitable for him. Apparently, we're the ones in danger of being forced out of the Liberty."

I scratched my head. "And that means you're speaking to me?"

"No, it means we know we can't compete with your resources. So we were hoping to play nice—nicer," Greta corrected herself.

"And find out the truth about Celia Preston!" Florence piped in. In their hearts, the Windsor sisters were terrible gossips. That might be what actually motivated them to get out of bed in the morning. "So, is it true? Did she kill her son's girlfriend?"

"I don't know, and I'm not going to comment," I said wearily. "And if you two think that interrogating me when we just got home after a long trip and a challenging afternoon is in any way going to dissuade me from buying you out, you're wrong. Good evening, ladies."

My arm protectively around Jenny's shoulders, I hustled us past them to the safety of the elevators.

"They need to get a life," Jenny correctly assessed after the elevator doors closed. "Also, did they say you're buying out their apartment?"

"Maybe. But the South End's sounding better and better."

"It'd be hard to find a nicer place than yours," Jenny said.

"True," I said as the elevator doors opened on my spectacular space. I did love the Liberty. "Maybe we don't need to get you a South End condo. Maybe you can just stay here with me."

I had intended to buy Jenny a place of her own, but now that we were home, it seemed nuts that she would be anywhere other than right by my side. All the time. Every day. Every night. In *our* home.

"Because really..." I scratched my head. "Why do we need two places?"

We looked at each other. Jenny opened her mouth and then closed it. I was about to say something—being me, I had no idea what—when my phone buzzed with a call from Shirley. "It's Shirley, I should take this. She'll be upset by seeing Celia Preston in the news."

Jenny nodded, heading into the bedroom to change out of her travel clothes.

"Mr. Bryson? Oh, Mr. Bryson, I'm so glad you picked up! I was so worried when I saw the news just now—"

"We're fine, Shirley," I assured her. "Jenny and I just got back to the Liberty."

"Did your father call you?" she asked.

"Not yet," I sighed. "But I had a few messages from Kevin while I was away. What's up? Did my father call *you*?"

"Yes, and he said some terrible things." To my horror, she sniffled, and I realized Shirley was crying. "He made some accusations about J-Jenny that were just awful. And he tried to force me to tell him what I knew about you two. Mike was so upset, he said I should quit—"

"Sorry, who's Mike?" I interrupted. I felt a dull headache coming on.

"My husband, Michael. You've met him, silly! Anyway, he said that I should quit because your father threatened me. And then I couldn't stop crying, but I said no way, not when Mr. Bryson finally met a nice girl!" She paused to blow her nose. "But that's the thing, your father was making up all sorts of lies about Jenny, things that were really unkind. And then he said he'd go after me if I didn't cooperate. So I told him where to go!"

She blew her nose again. "I didn't want to bother you when you were on your nice vacation, but I wanted to tell you as soon as you got back. I don't know what he's up to, but I know it's not good."

"Thank you, Shirley. I'm sorry you had to go through that. Take the rest of the week off, okay? You need a break. I'll be fine."

"Is Jenny with you? Is she okay?"

I was touched that Shirley already cared so much about my girlfriend. "Yes, she is. And don't worry about my father. I'm handling it, okay? I'm sorry he harassed you—I won't let that happen again."

We hung up, and I paced for a moment. My fucking father was a lunatic. He might not be Celia-Preston-level bad, but he was still an absolute ass. I needed to deal with him, but I had to gather my thoughts first. I couldn't believe he'd called my assistant and harassed her like that. It made me certain that the investigator sniffing around the Liberty had been hired by him, too. Part of me wanted to call him right then and there and have it out with him. But my father was shrewd, and he was always prepared. Going at him when I was off-balance and erratic wasn't in my best interest. I needed to be calm, rested, and clear-thinking when I approached him.

There was nothing I could do tonight. Resigned, I headed for the bedroom. I found Jenny in one of my T-shirts; she'd quickly changed and was unpacking. "I have someone who can do that, you know."

She looked confused. "Unpack? I think I can handle it."

"I just talked to Shirley," I sighed. I wanted to tell Jenny about my father, but I didn't want to make her upset. So instead, I asked, "Did you know she was married?"

"Yeah, of course. She and Michael have been together for fifteen years. They met later in life, ya know? She said he's a real good guy." Jenny nodded.

I shook my head. "I'm an ass, you know that?"

She laughed. "No Cole, I didn't. Watcha mean?"

"I mean, I didn't even remember that my assistant was

married. Shirley's worked for me forever. She said I've met him—I'm sure I have." I shrugged. "But when I think about Shirley, I'm never really thinking about Shirley. I'm thinking about *me*. What she can do for me, what she needs to do for me, etc."

Jenny nodded. "Like I said, buy her a gift."

"I told her to take the week off," I said semi-defensively.

"Ooh, even better. Send her and Michael on a cruise! They love cruises."

I watched as she separated out my clean tees from my dirty ones, put my clothes neatly back into the correct drawers, closed up the suitcase, and put it away. "How do you know that they like cruises?" I asked.

"Shirley and I were talking about vacations," she said as she unpacked the next suitcase. "She said she and Mike like to go cruising 'cause it's real relaxing. You don't have to go anywhere 'cause you're already somewhere, you know?"

She set our toiletries down carefully, then set the collection of shells she'd amassed on the dresser.

"Jenny, have I told you that I love you?" I asked.

She beamed at me as she folded and re-folded one of her bikinis. "Yeah, you have. And I'm real glad, 'cause I love you, too. Now buy Shirley a cruise, will ya? It's the least you can do for forgetting that she has a life outside work."

"I'm an ass," I said again.

"Nah," Jenny said with a grin. "You were doing your best. But now you can do better, right? So do it."

"Yes, Jenny. I will." I vowed, right then and there, to do better in all areas of my life.

But especially in the area she occupied, front and center.

I may never have been in love before, but I was sophisticated enough to know the real thing when I found it.

I HAD another one of my employees book a trip for Michael and Shirley. The trip, as Jenny said, was "wicked nice." The Ritz-Carlton cruise left from Boston and sailed to ports in Bermuda, Turks and Caicos, the Dominican Republic, and Puerto Rico. I had Jenny call her and deliver the good news. Even though I was in the kitchen, I could hear Shirley screaming through the phone.

"You did good with that cruise, Cole," Jenny said as we snuggled under the covers that night. "I even told Shirley it was your idea."

"Did she believe you?"

"Nah," Jenny laughed. "But she was so happy. She said Michael's eyes filled with tears because he was so glad she was bein' recognized for all her hard work."

"Ah, that's nice." I should've done it sooner.

As if she could hear my thoughts, Jenny patted me on the shoulder. "You could make it an annual thing, you know? Sending them on a nice trip? They'd probably never accept it, but you could still offer."

"She *did* get you those thong bikinis," I reasoned.

"Yeah, she did." Jenny yawned. "Shirley's the best, ya know?"

"I know." I kissed the top of her head. "And you don't let the best things in life go."

"True." She snuggled against me and murmured, "Love you."

My heart swelled. Despite the drama with Celia Preston and my father, I'd never been so happy in my life. "I love you, too."

I waited until she was asleep, then I crawled out of bed, padded out to the kitchen, and called my father. I'd planned on waiting, but I'd waited long enough. I was calm. I'd thought it through. Much like Shirley's vacation, the conversation was long overdue.

It was time for me to step up.

It was late, and he'd already be getting to bed, but I wanted to get this over with. Dad picked up after one ring. "What the hell do you want?" he snarled. "It's ten o'clock!"

"I wanted to talk to you," I said, "after my girlfriend was asleep."

"She's not your girlfriend. She's your *hooker*," he spat.

"Not anymore, Dad. I bought out her contract." I paused for a beat. "She's a civilian now. No more ties to the agency."

"Being a prostitute is like being a lawyer—you're always one, no matter what," he said. "I've looked into this girl. She has a background, son. She's not good for you."

"Everybody has a story, Dad," I sighed. "And you don't end up working at an agency like AccommoDating unless you've had a rough go of it. That doesn't make her a bad person. That doesn't make her bad for *me*."

"I think you need to hear me out on this. You know how strongly I feel," Dad warned.

"I'll meet with you to talk about it." He might change his tune when he saw I was sincere in my feelings for Jenny. I doubted it, but it was worth a shot—an appeal to any remaining decency was all I had.

"That's a good start. But I need you to know that I was serious about your inheritance," my father said. "What happens to our family legacy is not a joke."

I wanted to say that threatening to leave his money to my failed hockey coach and bitchy neighbors was, in fact, the real joke. But instead, I said, "Fine. In the interim, I'd like to ask that you stop threatening my staff and the people who work at my building. Harassment isn't a good look, Dad. Since you're so concerned with appearances, you might want to look in the mirror."

"I suggest that you worry about yourself," he countered. "You've never been in a relationship, son. You might think you're sophisticated, but have you considered that maybe you don't know what the hell you're doing?"

"Bye, Dad."

He didn't return the formality. He simply hung up.

I headed back to bed. I didn't feel much better, but at least I'd done something. I climbed under the covers next to Jenny's warm body, refusing to give my father another thought until absolutely necessary.

CHAPTER 33
Jenny

COLE WAS WORKING THAT MORNING. I DIDN'T even realize he had a home office until he showed me the vast room on the far side of the kitchen. We'd made plans to finally see a Thunder game that night. Cole said he'd already bought me a Thunder hoodie and that we would have the best time. I couldn't wait!

With a vow to come out of his meetings for lunch, he gave me a hot kiss. Then he reluctantly headed to his desk. I headed out to the kitchen, badly needing a coffee.

I hated to be apart from Cole for the rest of the morning, but it was likely for the best. I'd slept in and woken up feeling like I'd been hit by a truck. All those rum punches, tequila shots, and emotions from vacation seemed to have caught up with me. I didn't feel bad, especially, just tired. I had a lot on my mind. There was sifting and sorting to do, the need to figure out how Cole and I would make this work. It seemed easy enough. I'd already called Elena and quit. Next up was a call to my landlord, and then Cole and I needed to discuss whether or not he'd meant what he'd said about me moving into the Liberty.

When we first talked about our future, I'd thought he wanted to set me up in my own place. Then he'd kinda-sorta move in with me. It seemed that buying me my own condo was, in his mind, the next rational step. We'd only been dating for two weeks. We could still have some independent space if I had my own place. If I moved in with him here, we'd be officially official both internally and externally. Maybe that was too many adverbs for Coley to handle all at once.

But as soon as we'd gotten back to the Liberty, he seemed like he changed his mind. Like he wanted me to stay there and live with him full-time. Maybe he was already ready for more.

Was I?

The thing was, the answer seemed simple: I couldn't imagine being away from him. Why would I want my own place if it meant he might not be there? Why would I want my own bed when I liked sharing his? It had only been a short amount of time, and yet I felt like I no longer made sense without Cole. He'd become just as much a part of me as my curls and honking laugh; I wouldn't be me without him.

So I knew my answer, even though it scared the hell outta me.

It was yes. Yes, I was already ready for more.

I let myself sing a happy song in the shower, "Walking on Sunshine," an oldie but a goodie. And for the first time in a long time, I didn't berate myself for hoping. I let myself feel, once again, that perhaps my hope was meant to be. Maybe good things could happen. Even for a girl like me.

I was still humming the tune while I dressed. I heard my phone beep and lunged for it, hoping it was Audrey. I wanted to know if there was anything new with crazy-ass Celia Preston. But it was a text from an unknown number with a six-one-seven area code, someone local but unfamiliar.

> Funny to be seeing you so dressed up.

The sender included a screenshot of Cole and me walking into Todd and Evie's wedding. My head was held high. Cole was grinning, his arm around me in my special mermaid dress.

> Sluts like you don't deserve dresses like that.
>
> You can pretend, but I know the truth.
>
> Once a whore, always a whore.

I blinked at the messages. They were so mean. I felt like I'd been slapped in the face.

There was a girl who I used to work with, Renata, who was always picking on me—she was real jealous. Maybe this was her?

> Renata, is that you, you bitch?
>
> Don't you think it's time you got a life?

> It's not Renata. What kind of frickin' name is that, anyway?
>
> It's Aunty Theresa. Remember me?
>
> The one who took you in? When you had nothing? When no one else gave a shit?
>
> You stole from me, and you lied. And I ain't ever gonna forget about it, BITCH.
>
> I'M GONNA MAKE YOU PAY!
>
> You AND that billionaire of yours.

She included emojis of an eggplant, a bagful of money, and a devil face.

I didn't put my phone down—I threw it across the room. And then I ran into the bathroom and promptly threw up.

After I cleaned myself up, I took a deep breath and picked up my phone, even though I didn't want to. The screen was cracked, but I could still see I had a missed call. It was another local number, but it wasn't from my Aunty Theresa, thank goodness.

My phone flashed; I had a new voicemail. With shaking hands, I pressed the Play button.

"Jennifer, this is Lewis Bryson, Cole's father," said a man. His voice was deep, like Cole's, but icy. "I don't usually leave phone messages, but this communication required special consideration. Please listen carefully, as I'm not apt to repeat myself.

"I've been in contact with your family, in particular, your aunt. They know all about you. They also know about Cole. You might not care about my son, but I do," he said.

I clutched my stomach.

"Your aunt seemed very interested to hear you were dating a billionaire. She said that you owed her quite a large sum of money. She also said you'd done some things you should be ashamed of—things you might not want my son to know."

A cold sweat broke out on the back of my neck.

"Let me make this simple for you," Lewis Bryson said. "Leave now and don't look back. If you do that, I'll ensure your aunt stays where she should: at the bottom of the trash heap. But if you defy me and stay with my son, I am going to fund her smear campaign. Your choice, Jennifer. Please make the right one. If not for you, then for my son. You have until noon today to leave the Liberty. Don't say one word to Cole. Otherwise, there'll be hell to pay."

I didn't bother throwing the phone. This time, I just dropped it.

It took me a full minute to process what had happened. My Aunty Theresa had found me because Cole's father had found *her*. He knew all about me. He'd listened to the terrible things she'd said. He didn't want me anywhere near his son, and I couldn't blame him.

There was no question in my mind about what I was going to do.

There was only one way forward. There was only one way to survive this. *Run.* Running was the only reason I was still alive; I knew that. Being smart was my secret weapon, and I was smart enough to have learned the lesson when it was taught to me the hard way.

I looked at the clock. At twelve, Cole would come out looking for his lunch.

At twelve, I'd be long gone.

It was for the best. I was making the best choice for the man I loved.

Your choice, Jennifer, Lewis Bryson had said.

Please make the right one. If not for you, then for my son.

I'd never in a million years thought that my Aunty Theresa would come back. I'd thought she was dead. Poor lifestyle choices, ya know? But what I'd believed as a child had proven true: evil things didn't die. They were like scenes from a scary movie or monsters in your closet; that shit could haunt you forever.

I scrawled out a note for Cole.

Hey Cole:

I'm sorry, but I have to leave. I've been doing some thinking and this just isn't going to work. I'm not made for a real relationship. I can't really picture living here in this fancy building, acting like I'm on the same level as you. Or even at the same level as Florence and Greta. They're bitches, but they bought their own place, ya know?

I didn't do that. I won't ever be able to do that.

I don't belong here. I don't belong in your world.

I'm sorry I'm missing out on the box seats at the Thunder tonight. I was really looking forward to that.

I'll still root for your team, though.

The wedding was fun, the vacation was fun, staying at your swanky penthouse was fun. I loved every second. But you know what they say, right? All's well that ends well. It's better this way, Coley. You stay okay and I'll stay okay.

Okay?

We'll always have the seals. And Iggy the Iguana. I won't ever forget that dressing room, either, not to mention the plunge pool.

You're a good guy.

I know you'll make a nice girl real happy one day.

~ Jenny

I put the note on the table and grabbed my bag.

Then, without a backward glance, I left the Liberty—and Cole, and any chance of happiness I'd ever known—far, far behind.

I KNOW, I know—I am SO sorry about that cliffhanger, lol! Luckily, Book Two will be available soon! Cole and Jenny's epic love story continues in Book Two of *The Venture Capital Trilogy*!

You can find it here:

www.amazon.com

DID you know you can read James and Audrey's epic love story in *Escorting the Billionaire*? Find it here:

www.amazon.com

Thank you so much for reading! Lots of love to all of you!

xoxo

Leigh

About the Author

USA Today and Amazon Top-10 Bestselling Author Leigh James is currently sitting on a white-sand beach, watching the sunset, dreaming up her next billionaire. Get ready, he's going to be a HOT one!

Just kidding! Leigh is actually freezing her butt off in Maine, USA, where she lives with her awesome husband, their great kids, and her BFF Choco the chocolate lab. But she promises that billionaire is REALLY going to be something!

Leigh also writes Young Adult Paranormal Romance as Leigh Walker. Her smash-hit series *Vampire Royals* was previously optioned by Netflix. Her books have been translated into German, French, Italian, and Portuguese.

Thank you for reading. Lots of love to all of you!

Want to be the first to hear about new releases, free books, and other exclusive giveaways?

SIGN UP FOR MY NEWSLETTER!

— LJ —

Leigh James
USA Today Best-Selling Author
LeighJamesAuthor.com

Also by Leigh James

The Escort Collection

Escorting the Player

Escorting the Billionaire

Escorting the Groom

Escorting the Actress

Escorting the Royal

The Venture Capital Trilogy

The Billionaire and I (Book One)

Book Two

Book Three

The Forever Trilogy

The Forever Contract (Book 1)

The Forever Promise (Book 2)

The Forever Vow (Book 3)

~

Hot Fake Date

~

One Island Summer

~

Silicon Valley Billionaires

Book 1

Book 2

Book 3

~

The Liberty Series

Made in the USA
Middletown, DE
30 January 2024